A
DARK
AND
DISTANT
PLACE

How far would you go to find the truth about your parents?

A
DARK
AND
DISTANT
PLACE

PIERRE DELERIVE

SIMPLE SOLDAT

A retarded young man is drafted by
the French army during the Algerian
war. A soldier by accident, he dies a
hero by accident and in the process
changes the young men around him.

Le Figaro littéraire:

*"Pierre Delerive's novel is tough
and has muscle. His words
hit their mark. A spade is a
spade and these soldiers are in no need of intellectual
justifications."*

VICTOR ET LES FEMMES

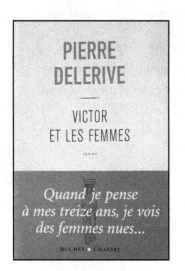

On the day of his mother's funeral, a middle-aged man remembers
his teen years struggling with his
exploding sexuality under her re-
gime of madness and terror.

Le Figaro Magazine :

*"Delerive's painting of the tran-
sition between childhood and
adolescence is a success. There
are beautiful portraits of wom-
en. Both tragic and hilarious."*

TE SOUVIENS-TU DE MOI?

In wartime Paris, a young man was once forced to choose between selling his best friend to the Nazis, or saving his Jewish lover. Years later a telephone call reminds him that the past cannot be buried.

Marie-Claire :

"Unforgettable. Impossible to put down. Awesome writing. In short – sorry for the superlatives – an unforgettable book."

In French and English Translation

LE PASSÉ MALGRÉ NOUS.

A native of Alsace, Roland was forced to serve in the German army. Late in life, he meets Claire, whose fiancé, a resistance fighter, was executed by the Nazis. The past finds a way back into their lives when Claire discovers that Roland hasn't told her the whole truth about his days as a German soldier.

Les dernières nouvelles d'Alsace :

"Relates with realism the cruel circumstances of the Frenchmen from Alsace and their difficult return home after the war ... Faithfully chronicles how many failed to understand those who had been forced to wear the hated uniform."

BAYOU CRUEL

Two strangers die at the same time: Toby, an old black man, is murdered near a Louisiana bayou; Arnaud, a Parisian restaurateur, is trapped in a fire. Resuscitated after several minutes of clinical death, Arnaud awakens inhabited by Toby's soul. Drawn to the place of the crime where he's haunted by a sense of déjà vu, he sets out to find the old man's murderer.

Télé 7 jours:

"The feeling of déjà vu is haunting. Danger!"

"For Toni, my wife and best friend"

Prologue

I often wonder what would have happened if I'd been scouting locations abroad when the telephone rang. Or if I'd simply told my father that I would be busy on a shoot for several weeks and suggested that he call a moving company instead. He was hardly the only old man in the world who had to sift through the relics of a lifetime. So many what ifs... all of them futile, I know, yet they haunt me every time I relive those events that – so harmless-seeming, at least to begin with – turned me into a murderer. Or perhaps even worse than a murderer, though I will never know that for sure. Not knowing is my choice.

I made no conscious effort to memorize the details of our conversation that evening, yet every word of it is engraved in my mind. It's all there, precise and detailed, and time has not even blurred its edges. With no effort at all, I can return to that moment on Saturday May 13, 2017, when we had just finished eating dinner.

Chapter One

We were on the cheese course when the telephone rang. "Just let the answering machine get it," I told Sophie, as she sprang to her feet.

"Ah, good evening, Raoul," Sophie said. "Yes, he's here. Just a minute..."

Lucie rolled her eyes. "You know Mom never listens to anyone!" she groaned, with the world-weariness of a sixteen-year-old.

I sighed and pushed my plate away, then got to my feet. "It could have waited," I muttered as Sophie passed me the receiver.

"Be nice to him. He's probably fragile, after everything that's happened!"

Sophie is not one to hold a grudge. Her heart is more generous than mine.

"Hello, Dad!"

My father announced that he had finally decided to sell the apartment on Rue de la Roquette. He had somehow managed to get over the tragedy that had ended his marriage, but endlessly roaming those rooms with all their accumulated memories kept dragging him back into his depression.

"I got a good price for it," he told me cheerily. "And now I have to move."

"Really?"

"Don't act so surprised. You're the one that kept nagging me to move out. You even started on the day of the funeral!"

"Well, I think it's the right decision, obviously, but I can't believe you never even mentioned it to me. Even last Saturday--"

"Oh, because I need your permission, do I? I'm not senile yet, you know!"

I had become used to his aggressiveness over the years. I knew he was not about to change.

"Of course not. I was just expecting to have a talk about where you'll live next. I imagine you're considering your options. Do you want to discuss it?"

"I've made my decision. I signed the papers yesterday. I'll be living in a senior residence in the southern suburbs."

I thought about Sophie, who had asked me the previous evening where I got my stubborn streak from.

The fact that my father had even made this phone call was an event in itself. He belongs to a generation that remembers when such calls were expensive, and generally prefers to wait for me to call him, concealing this reflex under the pretense that he "doesn't want to disturb" me.

I tried to control my frustration. "The southern suburbs…. All right, Dad. Anything else?"

"Well, I was calling because I was wondering…."

He let the last word hang. Whatever he was going to ask me was costing him.

"Wondering what?"

"If you might be free one weekend to help me go through

everything. I can't take it all with me. There won't be enough space anyway. So, I have to move all that stuff out of the cellar, pack it in boxes, figure out what I should sell or give away… you see what I mean?"

"A weekend. When?"

"Well, I say a weekend, but to be honest, there's a huge mess down there. A lifetime of belongings. So, I don't really know how long it will take… Philippe, are you still there?"

"Yes, Dad, I'm just thinking. If you give me the dates, I can probably take a week off work. That'd be more practical, don't you think?"

So that is how I come to be in the Bastille neighborhood this Monday morning at the wheel of a van borrowed from Studio Plus. I know my father; there are bound to be objects that he would not want to be handled by a professional moving company, and I am determined to satisfy all his whims. When he mentioned that "my room" was ready for me, I realized that I would probably never get another opportunity like this. "You want to be a good boy for Daddy," Sophie had told me with a smile.

She was right, but there was more to it than she knew. Yes, it was true that I wanted to be the model son that I had not been when I was younger, in order to create a memory that would survive my father, but more than that I wanted to – not erase, because that would be impossible – but at least heal the wounds from the act of violence that had kept us estranged for nearly two years.

I had just completed my first feature film as a cinematographer – five weeks in Normandy and three in Italy – and, during the flight back to Paris, had been warmly congratulated and promised similar work in the future. Proud at having passed this test, I jumped in a taxi at the airport and decided to pay a surprise visit to my parents. I wanted them to know that I had found my way in life.

I always kept a copy of the keys to the apartment where I grew up, just in case anything happened and they needed my help. I let myself in that day, already anticipating their joy at my unexpected presence, and called out "Mom! Dad! It's me!" It was late in the evening, so I rushed to my parents' room, expecting to find them in bed, watching their favorite TV show.

My mother was alone there in the darkness. Her head resting on a pillow, she was holding a towel to her face. At first, she resisted when I tried to move her hand out of the way, then she let me do it. I turned on the bedside lamp and gasped. I will never forget the sight of her beat-up face. Her left eye was almost swollen shut, and her cheek was purple.

"Mom! What happened?"

"I fell. It's not as bad as it looks."

"But... where's Dad?"

The fear I saw in her eyes led me to suspect the truth. I knew all too well the violence that inhabited my father, having witnessed his furious fits of rage on several occasions. Once I saw him punch a hole through the wall between the kitchen and the corridor; another time, he smashed a chair against my bedroom door because I'd put a few stickers on it. I retained a vivid memory of the spankings he would give me with his belt and, of course, the unforgettable beating that had left me bleeding on my bathroom floor. But never before had he raised his hand to my mother.

"Tell me the truth, Mom."

"It was my fault. I'd told him I was going to eat dinner with Céline, a friend from the hospital, and I gave him her phone number because he always insists I do that. But one of the digits was wrong, and when he called the number, he found himself talking to a stranger. He accused me of lying to him, of spending the evening with another man, but you know that I--"

I stopped listening. I strode angrily toward the kitchen, where I found my father sitting at the table, head between his hands, an empty glass and an almost empty bottle of wine in front of him.

'You did that to her?

I had to shake him by the shoulders and repeat my question several times before he replied in a toneless voice "She lied to me."

That night, I learned that I too was capable of a violent rage. Grabbing the rolling pin from the draining board, I raised it above my father's head and heard myself yell "You ever touch her again, and I'll beat the living hell out of you."

He leapt to his feet, shoved away the chair, and stood facing me. My words, and the tone of my voice, had woken some monster deep within him.

"Go ahead and try," he growled. "If you're man enough."

How many times have I relived that moment, as rage overcame me and I swung that length of solid wood at my father's head? I still can't believe how fast his reflexes were. With the faintest movement of his legs, his hips, he casually ducked out of the way.

In an instant, my fury evaporated and I was left with the horrified realization of what I had almost done. I dropped the rolling pin on the floor, turned on my heel, and ran back to my mother. She refused to answer my questions. All she would say, in a whisper, was that it was "her fault too." She let me rub some antiseptic cream on the cut on her cheek and put a compress to her eye. In the end, she fell asleep in my arms. As I left the apartment, I glimpsed my father sitting at the table, head buried in his arms.

I didn't see him again for almost two years. Every week, when I was in Paris and when my work allowed, I would meet my mother in a café near the Saint Antoine hospital where she worked. This café, Les Blouses Blanches, was her favorite. She reassured me that everything was fine again with my father. Not only had he begged her forgiveness and sworn that never would such a "monstrous" act (the word was his) be repeated, but he had decided never to touch another drop of alcohol.

"He poured all the wine out of the bottles into the sink," my mother told me one day, her voice full of admiration. "All of them, in one night. Can you believe it? Sometimes, when we go to eat dinner at Vittorio's, I notice that he's eyeing the wine menu. I tell him, you can have a glass or two, you know, it's not going to hurt. But no, he hasn't forgiven himself."

She took my hand in hers as she concluded "And if I've forgiven him, I think you can too. Come and have dinner with us."

But I wasn't ready. "I need more time, Mom."

"Why?"

"I can't explain it. This whole thing really affected me. I feel traumatized. But…one day soon, I promise."

I wasn't being entirely honest. What scared me most was my own nature. I had spent my childhood and adolescence idolizing my father, but also fearing him. Now I was terrified that I might have inherited the darkest depths of his temperament. The blood that flowed through our veins was poisoned, I felt sure of it.

Then came my mother's fiftieth birthday. "Come on, do it for me," she pleaded. "Your father would be so pleased, too. I promise you, everything will be fine. I'll make my gratin dauphinois for you."

"Your *gratin*! Why didn't you say that before? We've wasted two years."

"One year and eleven months. So…what would you like for dessert?"

That birthday meal marked the end of our cold war, and the incident was never mentioned again. Which does not mean that my father or I ever forgot it, simply that, to quote his favorite saying, "That's life. You just have to get on with it."

Our relationship went back to normal, but it remains shallow. When did the two of us ever have a real conversation, an exchange of thoughts and ideas beyond the practical problems of everyday life? A plumber's invoice, his old car's engine troubles, the annual meeting of the apartment owners in his building…yes, we talked about all of that. But our hopes, regrets, dreams, ambitions and disappointments, our loves and friendships? Never. Not once. But, who knows, perhaps we will this week. Never have the two of us spent any time alone together. I can only hope that our demons will not awaken each other.

—⊸∞⊷—

The apartment where my parents lived for more than forty years, and where I grew up, is located close to Boulevard

Voltaire, on the fifth and top floor of a gray building that, I can now see, is completely bereft of charm or originality. It has changed very little over the years. The old couple who used to act as concierges were replaced by a generously proportioned female caretaker in a turban and multicolored robes. The double doors are now opened by a code. Letters are no longer delivered to each floor but left in tiny mailboxes in the lobby. Other than this sullen modernization and the exotic smells of the meals being cooked behind the caretaker's door, the building is essentially unchanged. There is still something sepulchral about the stairwell, dimly lit by the rays of daylight filtered through the dusty windows.

The modernization does not extend to the elevator which is more run-down than ever, all attempts to refurbish it having failed to pass a majority vote at the annual owners' meeting. According to my father, those meetings are mostly an opportunity for people who do not speak a word to one another all year long to air their accumulated grievances. My father has a nickname for each of the other owners. There's "Ole and Axel" on the first floor, "the hare and the tortoise" on the second, "la cage aux folles" (actually two gay men) on the third, and the "kikes" on the fourth.

My father sometimes wonders what nickname they have for him. "If I were you," I told him one day, "I wouldn't want to know."

My parents could not afford the apartment of their dreams when they first moved to Paris. My father had been appointed assistant manager for a new branch of the furniture store where he worked in Nice. When he came to Paris, he was horrified by the cost of rentals. Miraculously, one of his saleswomen offered him the solution. Her aunt, a woman in her seventies with financial worries, had decided to divide her apartment on Rue de la Roquette and to rent out the other two rooms.

"That's probably why you're an only child," my father told me one day. "That dividing wall was so thin that we could hear her turn the pages of her romance novels and sniff when the emotion got too much for her. So…well, that stole our thunder a bit when it came to the noises we made, if you know what I mean."

Their early years were difficult. My father did not want his wife to work. Born to a wealthy family in Clermont-Ferrand, she had not been raised in a world of typists, saleswomen, and receptionists. Years would pass before he let her study for her nursing qualifications.

My father had just been promoted to the position of the store's manager when our landlady did not wake up one morning; her two children accepted a reasonable offer, and we were able to stay in the same apartment, with the aid of a mortgage. I still have a vivid memory of the jubilation we felt as we smashed down that dividing wall. I was allowed to drink my first mouthful of champagne that day, and I can still see my mother waltzing in the rubble of the living room as my father begged her to keep still for a moment so he could take a photograph.

Flattened cardboard boxes are piled up on the doorstep. "The moving company just delivered them," my father announces as he opens the door. On the floor are a couple of sky-blue paper slippers like I've seen in Japan, where no shoes are allowed on tatamis. "What's that for, Dad?"

"That, as you say, are slippers. What did you think they are? The repairman who came last month to fix the dishwasher had dog shit on his shoes and I had to clean it all up after he left. So, now, nobody walks in with their shoes. And when I say nobody, I mean nobody."

With his finger pointed at my boots, my father makes sure his message has been delivered. I bite my tongue and shrug. It's only for a few days. I am immediately struck by the odor of tobacco that pervades the air of the apartment. My father is now living like a bachelor.

I follow him through the hallway that leads to my bedroom and a wave of confused emotion washes over me. I was only six when we moved to Paris, so any memories I have of that time are echoes of stories that my mother told me later. She was a born storyteller and I used to spend hours at her feet, my cheek resting on her nylons, listening fascinated as she stroked my head and told me about her childhood. She had a soft, deep, melodious voice, which would tremble with emotion when she described the life she lived before meeting my father: a life of luxury and sophistication in a magnificent mansion with the number of bedrooms and bathrooms that I could only imagine in a palace. She had a beautifully designed garden with a number of flowerbeds, a swimming pool and a tennis court. The majordomo, a silver-haired, white-gloved, stern-looking gentleman, ruled over a staff of maids, cooks, chauffeurs, and gardeners.

One woman, Layla, was Mother's exclusively, from the moment she came to her room to pull the curtains open to the end of the day when she chose a nightgown for her, tucked her in, and read a couple of chapters of her favorite books before switching off the lights. She rarely talked about her parents who, though loving and generous, were too deeply engaged in family affairs and busy with lavish receptions to spend much time with their daughter. Years later, when I watched *Gone With the Wind* for the first time, I felt as if that world of gentlemen and beautiful ladies in crinolines was the American version of the world my mother had evoked for me.

My memory darkens as the sweetness of those moments listening to my mother is disturbed by the sudden remembrance of her mood swings. Her descents into what she herself called her own private hell would always fill me with dread and sadness.

My father's childhood was much darker than my mother's, as I learned one evening. I was eight or nine years old then, and it is still the only time I ever heard him share memories of his younger years, helped as he was that day by a copious intake of his Postillon cheap red wine.

I had followed my mother to the kitchen, where she had prepared a cup of my favorite treat: a thick, creamy, dark chocolate mousse. My father was seated at the kitchen table, staring at a newspaper. He wasn't reading it; he just stared at it. An empty glass was sitting between two bottles of wine.

"Raoul, honey, drinking that much isn't good for you, you know that," my mother had said pointing at the bottles.

"That one was half-empty," my father had slurred.

With a sigh, my mother had left the kitchen while I sat on a stool at the table with my cup of mousse.

I don't remember what prompted my father to speak, nor

the exact words he used, but the extraordinary experience of my father sharing intimate memories was so startling that I still have a vivid recollection of that evening.

The newspaper article that had caught his attention was about the discovery of a teenager's body in a garbage dump. He had been strangled and stabbed several times for good measure, and in his pants pocket a diary had been found where he had scribbled accounts of his mistreatment at the hands of the foster family he had fled, detailing descriptions of all the beatings and humiliations he had endured. The article included a photo of one page of the diary, and as I read it afterwards, I was struck by the fact that the handwriting was that of a child rather than a young man.

The fact that the victim was a runaway had shaken my father, and he suddenly, started talking about his own childhood. His eyes fixed on the newspaper in front of him, he never looked up and seemed completely unaware that I was listening. His voice was deeper than usual and his words came out slowly, his tongue heavy with alcohol.

This is how I learned that my father had been placed in three homes after being left as a baby on the steps of a church. He didn't say much about the first two families or how they were selected, but he shared some bitter memories of the last one. He, like the child in the newspaper article, had been bullied, harassed, beaten, and humiliated by the twenty-year old, body-building son of the family and his younger sister, while the mother and father orchestrated the show and laughed.

It had started the first evening in this new home. Having been shown to his room, a dank basement where an old mattress on the concrete floor and a couple of dirty blankets awaited him, he had come upstairs to sit at the dinner table, where he was assigned a stool. Everybody else sat on a chair. The first course was a thick soup of vegetables with morsels of meat. He had not eaten since the morning and was starving, but he was denied seconds as the father, son, and daughter helped themselves to a generous second plate. Only one serving for him, that was the rule, the mother had said while son and daughter nodded approvingly.

The chores assigned to him had been laid out after dinner, and he was given an alarm clock to ensure an early start at 5:00 in the morning. While everybody else was still sleeping, he was to light the fire in the chimney when the weather turned cold, set up the breakfast table, clean all the shoes and boots, turn on the coffee maker and feed the dog—a German shepherd.

His days were busy. As soon as he came back from school, a three-mile walk, he had to wash the family pickup truck, clean the gutters and rake the leaves in the fall, bring the wood into the house in winter, pump air into the tires of the family bikes, all the while hearing the loud banter and laughter of the son and daughter watching sports on TV.

To celebrate his fifteenth birthday, my father had spent the money earned from mowing the neighbors' lawn on a small cake that he intended to enjoy before bedtime in his basement room. He had also bought fifteen small candles. He was in the process of lighting them when the brother and sister from hell, as he called them, as if informed by some evil, had surprised him. While the boy held my father's hand behind his back, his sister had forced his face into the cake. "T'was Happy birthday to me," groaned my father as I listened, horrified.

"Where did you get that money?" the mother had asked when my father complained about the attack. Upon learning that he had earned it, the mother had slapped him in the face. "You know damn well that you should have given me the money," she had yelled. "After all that we do for you!"

"That was it," said my father with a sad laugh, still staring at the newspaper. "The following day, I was gone. I found some money in the old harpy's handbag, took one of the bicycles from the shed, and left in the middle of the night with a shirt, a pair of jeans, and my toothbrush in the son's backpack. At least I didn't finish like the poor bugger in the newspaper."

"Where did you go, Dad?"

Mesmerized by what I had heard, I had forgotten to be afraid. As my father looked up, I saw that he was surprised to see me. Instead of glaring at me and ordering me back to my room, he shrugged his shoulders, with the shadow of a smile in his eyes, and continued.

"I rode all night until I reached a small town called Blanzat. It was still dark, but I saw a café where a man was preparing for his early customers. I walked in, ordered a cup of coffee, and went to sit at a table. When the man brought me the cup, he found me sound asleep. He sat down and asked me where I lived. Hearing that I really had no place to go, he took me to a room in the back where there was a cot surrounded by stacks of crates. That was the place where he liked to take a nap during the day.

I slept all day and woke up when he brought me a sandwich and a glass of lemonade. His name was Jeannot and he was the owner. He was bald, carried quite a paunch, and tufts of white hair sprouted from his nostrils, but his smile was the sweetest thing I had seen in quite some time. I felt safe with him, so I had no problem answering his questions. When I told him my story, he shook his head, patted my knee, and told me that I could stay as long as I wanted. He had reached the door when he turned around, a finger in the air, and told me that one of his two waitresses was about to get married and would be leaving soon. 'Do you think you could learn to wait the tables?' he asked. That moment was when I was allowed to finally start my life."

That was all for the night. My father was about to fill up his glass, but he changed his mind. "You go back to your room, now," he said, sounding both relieved of a burden and exhausted.

The following day, his mood had returned to its dark and sour default mode, and I never dared mention an evening that I knew I would never forget.

The door to the bedroom that used to be my parents' is ajar and I can see the dark-red velvet armchair still in its place under the room's only window. This sight brings back painful memories. I often used to watch my mother sit there motionless in the darkness, curtains drawn, lamps off, withdrawn into a world that did not admit me. No matter what I did to attract her attention – bombard her with questions, clown around, pretend I had toothache, even once cut my thumb with a razor blade and show her my blood-covered hand – nothing made any difference. Her eyes, when they happened to alight on me, stared straight through me. In those moments, I did not exist for her, and that made me despair. I was always deeply affected by those moods of hers when she would shut herself away in a dark and mysterious inner world, sometimes for hours on end.

There were meals during which not a single word was spoken. It no longer hurts to remember those evenings when my father, jaws tensed, eyes glaring, would nurse one of his cold rages while my mother – having used up all her remaining energy simply by coming to the table – would sit there, absent and silent. I have wept enough over all of that.

As for the circumstances of my mother's death, I still try not to think about it.

"You remember where your room was, don't you? We used it as a storeroom, but I've tidied it up for you."

It has been years since I have been here, in my childhood bedroom. When I used to visit my parents – and then, later, my father – I never felt any need to retrace my steps.

I pause for an instant in the doorway, surprised by a brief surge of emotion, then walk into the room. Nothing has changed, even if it is much smaller than in my memories. I recognize the striped wallpaper, the white wooden chest of drawers, the little desk and its stool, the crucifix above the bed, but I am taken aback by how narrow and cramped it feels.

I drop my bag on the bed. My eyes rest on the nightstand where I once carved my initials. The memory of the punishment I received that day comes back to me too.

I walk over to the window. From this side, there is a view of the rooftops of two four-story buildings. One of these roofs had been transformed into a terrace, surrounded by a wire mesh fence intended to protect it from indiscreet glances. From my elevated observation post, I had a unique view. Every year, I would eagerly await the return of the summer heat because it would bring with it the reappearance of a woman whose face I would be incapable of describing, but whose body used to drive me wild with lust. A bleached blonde, the same age as my parents, this woman would saunter onto the roof terrace just before noon, so I could only enjoy the sight on Sundays or during school vacations. Dressed in a brightly colored bikini, she would lie on a towel and put a basket on the ground containing tubes of creams and lotions, and a bottle of water. I remember the rush I would feel when she took off her bra and prepared her body for sunbathing. I would imagine my hands, plastered with Ambre Solaire, moving over those magnificent breasts, and suddenly I would be unable to breathe. My throat would tighten, my erection would twitch in my hand. My bedroom door did not have a lock or even a bolt, so I had to keep my ears pricked for the sound of my mother's heels in the hallway even as my imagination swept me into a delirium of erotic fantasies.

The terrace has been transformed into a sort of greenhouse, behind whose windows can be seen various palm trees and bushes. I spot a brightly colored bird perched on a branch. It's like a tiny piece of the Amazon rainforest in the middle of the eleventh arrondissement.

"She's not there anymore," my father says, behind me. "She left a long time ago."

I turn around. "Who?"

He laughs. "You think you were the only one who used to stand there with his nose pressed to the window? Well, I say nose…"

He trails off, satisfied at having scored a point, then turns and leaves the room.

17

———⟨∞⟩———

I find my father in the kitchen. Standing next to the white-painted wooden table, he is busy making sandwiches. I lean against the side of the refrigerator and watch. I have not really observed him like this in years. His shoulders and back are a little more hunched than they were, but he is still a tall, solid-looking man. He started shaving his head once his hair began to recede, but his bushy eyebrows are still as black as the hair on his head used to be. The scar that runs down his right cheek is pale. My father has eaten mostly junk food since he became a widower and has grown a little plump, but with his six-foot frame the weight gain is hardly noticeable. The fingers of his right hand are yellowed by nicotine. He stopped wearing suits and ties long ago, and today he is in a wool shirt with the sleeves rolled up, and a pair of corduroy pants that conceal his belly. Of all the contradictory emotions that I feel, looking at him, in that moment the one that dominates is tenderness. It surprises me like a forgotten taste, a scent that I have not breathed in for many years.

He looks up. "What?"

"Nothing, Dad. I'm just watching you make sandwiches."

He is about to say something, but his gaze is caught by something behind me. I recognize the pinch of his lips, the glimmer of exasperation in his eyes that used to presage a volley of abuse or the slamming of a fist on the table. Today he is content to walk past me into the hallway to turn off the light that I have left burning there.

My father has waged a one-man war against wastefulness all his life. You should turn off a light when you leave a room, you should never leave a faucet running, you should finish all the food on your plate. For him, every penny counts and always will.

He catches me smiling when he comes back into the kitchen.

"What's so funny?"

"Nothing, Dad. I'm just remembering, that's all."

"Shame you didn't remember to turn off the lights."

I let him have the last word. He has no way of knowing that my assistants have learned to their cost not to let a generator keep running during a prolonged break, nor that Lucie has been trained to always turn off the light in her bedroom when she goes out. And that if she doesn't finish her meal, the leftovers will still be waiting for her in the fridge.

I continue my inspection. The rough patch of plaster is still visible on the wall where my father covered up the gaping hole left by his fist. I was thirteen or fourteen at the time. A stranger had asked to speak to my mother and said that his call was "confidential"; my father had hung up, then accused my mother of infidelity. "One of your lovers," he had yelled, before taking out his anger on the kitchen wall.

When my mother had brought back a note from one of the hospital's doctors the next day, confirming that he had wanted to inform her about the results of a patient's tests, my father had merely shrugged.

"What are you muttering about?"

"Nothing, Dad. I told you, I'm just remembering. It's kind of weird, coming back here to live."

"To live? Let's not exaggerate!"

My father turns away and bends down to open a drawer. He takes out two plates. In the mirror above the cupboard, I see him grimace with pain as he touches his lower back with his free hand.

"Are you in pain?"

Suddenly he stands up, as if jolted with a shock of electricity, and barks "Did you hear me complain?"

"No, of course not, you never complain. But there's no point suffering if you don't have to. There are pills you could take…"

He glances at me contemptuously and says "That's for pussies. I can handle a little pain." Then he turns back to his slices of ham and cheese. "I'm making us a snack. We're going to take some boxes to the new place, if that's all right with you?"

Without waiting for my response, he points with his knife at the hooks above the dishwasher. I see some keys hanging there.

"In the meantime, why don't you take a look in the cellar? First key on the left. It'll give you some idea of how much work we have to do."

As I leave the kitchen, he calls out "I hope you're not scared anymore."

As a child, I used to hate going down into that cavernous basement, with its dim bulbs and its seeping walls. I retain a horrible memory of the day when, bending down to tie my shoelaces, I let my father go up the stairs ahead of me, and he slammed the door shut just as the timer switch plunged me into darkness. How old was I then? Eight? Nine? Trying to find my way, I reached out to touch the wall, but my fingers grasped only a spiderweb. My heart stopped beating. The terror that filled me was so total that I couldn't even cry out. It took me months, perhaps years, to truly get over that day, and I remember my reaction, even as a young adult, when I was asked to go down to the cellar to fetch a bottle of wine. I obeyed, of course, and did my best to conceal my repugnance, but I could see in my father's eyes that he knew how it made me feel and that this knowledge gave him a sadistic pleasure. I hated him then.

Well, at least the lighting is better now. The padlock on the door is rusted but finally gives in. I come to a standstill in the doorway because there is nowhere else to go now. The entire room is filled to the ceiling with wooden trunks, old suitcases and cardboard boxes on which are written "crockery," "videos," "beach," "shoes," "kitchen," "Mom's clothes," and many other labels. There is a lamp with a dented shade. I can even see the high chair I used as a baby. All that's missing is *Citizen Kane's* sled – "Rosebud."

Taking a step back, I contemplate this incredible pile of junk, the sediment of half a century of lives, and think about something my spelunking friend Felix once said, when I went with him to the funeral of one of his teammates, who had died in a cave in Turkey: "It's true, it can be really goddamn dangerous," he sighed. "And yet…"

"And yet what?"

"When you go down into the darkness, you never know what you're going to discover."

———————

After returning from the cellar, I undress in my bedroom and walk through into the narrow en-suite bathroom. The shower is as feeble as ever.

Despite all the years that have passed, every detail of this room is familiar to me, from the magnifying mirror – dating from the first hairs to sprout from my chin – to the tooth-brush-glass holder patched up with duct tape, not forgetting the left-hand door of the cabinet that still doesn't close properly.

But my gaze is instantly riveted to one of the wall tiles. All of the tiles are decorated with images of nature – this one features a seagull against the background of a blue sky – but my attention is drawn inexorably to the upper right-hand corner, which was stuck back to the wall following an incident that is as raw in my memory as if I had just lived through it.

I was giving myself a quick wash that morning when my father burst into the room behind me, holding up a sheet of paper bearing the letterhead of my middle school. He had just opened the mail and discovered that I had been summoned to a meeting of the disciplinary council for fighting with a boy from the grade ahead of me. The boy's glasses had been broken and he had bled from a cut above his eyebrow, causing his parents to lodge a complaint, which meant that I would probably be expelled, particularly as this was not my first fight.

I tried to justify myself. That fat lying jerk had provoked me, accusing me of having gone through his schoolbag while it was lying in the courtyard at the foot of a tree. Without even bothering to listen to me, my father pressed the letter against the wall with one hand, and with the other mashed my face into it. 'You see what you did, you little prick?' he growled, before

22

grabbing a fistful of my hair and banging my head against the wall. 'Now you're going to have to change schools again! And always for the same dumb reason!'

He kept hammering my skull against the tile and the letter became spotted with blood, but by some miracle I did not lose consciousness. When my father's rage finally wore itself out and he left me alone on the bathroom floor, I slowly got to my feet and noticed that the wall was splattered with dark-red stains. As for the tile where he had held the letter, it was broken.

At the time, I don't think I realized the significance of this outpouring of violence. Reliving it like this makes me understand just how fully I have inherited my father's fatal flaw, a flaw I have struggled so hard to conquer. Sometimes, in a rage, when I have to force myself to unball my fists and breathe more slowly, I have the feeling that I am returning from some dark and distant place.

There have been times when I have hated my father, but that is an emotion I can no longer afford. My mother's death – and, in particular, the circumstances of her death – changed everything.

Chapter Two

Traffic is crazy on the Paris beltway the day after the long weekend. I turn to my father and see him checking his watch. "Good thing we don't have an appointment," I say. "God knows how long we're going to be stuck in this shit...."

He nods and mechanically pulls a packet of Gitanes from his shirt pocket. He catches me looking at him and puts it back.

"Sorry, Dad, but this isn't my vehicle, and Studio Plus is leading an anti-smoking campaign."

"No problem."

"So... why did you choose the south of Paris?"

He shrugs.

This gesture transports me years back in time, to when I used to desperately seek some solid ground between the shifting sands of my mother's depressive episodes and my father's impenetrable silences. He seemed to build an invisible wall around himself that insulated him from her black moods. Sooner or later, my mother would return to normal, aided by her collection of pills, but my father would remain in his fortress for hours afterward.

As we loaded the van, I asked him why we were taking sheets, blankets, a pillow, and toiletries with us. Aren't the movers paid for doing that? I had to repeat my question before he deigned to answer me. On the day the movers stripped his apartment bare, he would jump in his little Renault and wait for them at the Résidence Bellevue. "But you never know," he added.

He is a man who has always believed in being ready for the unexpected. What if the van broke down or was involved in a crash, for example, and his belongings were not delivered until a day or two later? My father would not be caught off guard, because today we are transporting everything he needs to equip his new apartment for a few nights. Just in case.

I do not reveal to him that the crew's nickname for me is "Plan B." Things can change quickly on a shoot, you see: the forecast sun might not appear; the lights and reflectors might not work. Anything might go wrong, so I try to be ready. Just in case.

As we approach the Porte de Bercy, the traffic on the beltway is transformed into a vast parking lot. Nothing moves. An ambulance and a fire truck speed past along the shoulder, sirens screaming, lights flashing. We are stuck. I have no Plan B.

"You may as well open the sandwiches," I say. "We're not going anywhere for a while."

As if he has not heard this, my father says simply "Thank you, Philippe."

'Thank you for what?'

'For taking this week off work.'

I find it hard to believe that those words really came out of his mouth. Not that I attach such importance to them, but my doubt reflects the ambiguities of our relationship. While my mother's effusiveness was sometimes so excessive that it made me uncomfortable, my father's coldness, his seething anger, his lack of spontaneity kept me continually off-balance.

"No problem, Dad. My next shoot has been put back anyway. A financing problem, just for a change."

I am lucky enough to be one of the few cinematographers – the official term, Director of Photography, has always sounded a bit pompous to me – with a reputation strong enough to keep him constantly employed. My father has never congratulated me on this success – that is not his way – but I assume that he is proud of me. Or at least satisfied with my material situation.

Two more ambulances howl past.

"Let's see if there's any news about this mess on the radio," I say, flicking from one station to the next. A woman's voice announces that traffic on the Paris beltway is backed up for six miles, and then they return to the studio for a discussion. It sounds unusually animated, so I keep listening. "Nonsense!" protests one of the participants. "How can anyone understand a person who does that? Suicide is an act against nature. Killing oneself, choosing death, is not a natural decision. Anyone who…"

My hand jerks toward the dashboard at the same time as my father's. Our fingers brush as I turn off the radio. From the corner of my eye, I watch my father pretending to be interested in the caravan standing motionless next to our van. His big hands lie tensed on his brown corduroy pants.

I am going to have to bite the bullet, conquer my fear of ruining these few days with my father. My mother's suicide would be less hard to bear if I could at least understand what led to it, I feel sure of that. She did not leave a note, and my father's stubborn insistence that he is as clueless about the cause as I am has never convinced me. It is true that my mother was prone to episodes of depression, but never, not once, did she talk about ending her life. Not in front of me, anyway. I find it hard to accept that her husband of almost fifty years does not at least have a theory.

Association of ideas. My best friend in high school, Francis, shot himself in the head. It happened after we had graduated, when Francis and I no longer saw much of each other. I heard the news through a mutual friend.

"What?" my father asks, without tearing his eyes away from the caravan.

"What do you mean, what?"

"That sigh."

I must have let my memories overwhelm me.

"Oh, I was thinking about Francis. My friend from high school. You remember him?"

He nods.

"His father was a piece of work," I say. "A red-faced giant who was always smiling and kind to his customers, but a bastard to his wife and his son."

"The butcher's shop has closed. It's a hairdressing salon now."

So, my father does not know about Francis's suicide. Or, more likely, he does not want to talk about it.

With its awning over the three glass entrance doors, the pillars to either side, and the thin young man in a dark gray uniform standing outside, the Résidence Bellevue puts me in mind of a four-star hotel that has been transformed into a retirement home due to declining business. Surely I am wrong, though. Who would ever build a hotel in such a bleak place?

The porter reluctantly walks over to us and helps us load our bags and suitcases onto a luggage cart. We follow him through the wide automatic doors, then my father heads toward the reception desk at the far end of the vast lobby while I observe the handful of residents.

Two women dressed in curiously identical suits sit chatting on fake leather ottomans. Their freshly permed hair shines in two different shades of silverish blue. A man whose face I cannot see – only his back and his shaved head – studies the small ads pinned to a corkboard with extreme attentiveness. As he reads them, he moves a few inches to the side every minute or so. A very frail old man emerges from the elevator, holding on to the arm of a robust black woman in a pink blouse. A young, athletic-looking woman talks into her cell phone while trying to calm down overexcited toddlers – visitors, without a doubt.

My father waves me over to the elevator. The porter is waiting for us with our luggage outside the door to room 606. My father uses his brand-new keycard to enter the apartment. I follow him in and find myself looking through a bay window that opens onto a narrow balcony. The dark sky and the pouring rain do nothing to brighten up the landscape.

"What do you think?" my father asks.

"I'm wondering why they call this place Bellevue. The view doesn't look too beautiful from here."

"Well, 'view of the train depot' doesn't have quite the same ring."

"What about the apartment buildings on either side?"

"They're going to be demolished."

"So why did you choose this place?"

"It was recommended to me. The restaurant's supposed to be good. I don't really care about the view."

I am about to point out that he has never seemed to care much about food either when the telephone on the wall starts to ring.

"Already!" my father grumbles.

I hear him reply in monosyllables, before announcing that he is going downstairs. "I have to see the manager," he says. "Papers to sign."

The air smells of fresh paint and the furniture in the living room is visibly new. An Ikea label hangs from the back of one of the chairs. A hallway leads to a bedroom, occupied for now by nothing more than a box-spring and a bare mattress. There is an alarm on the wall.

I find the bag containing the sheets, a blanket, and a pillow. As I am making the bed, I think about what Sophie said and smile; she was right – I do want to be a good little boy.

A telephone on the wall next to the bed starts to buzz. How many phones are there in this little apartment? I hesitate for a moment, then pick up the receiver.

"Hello?"

"Mr. Lamont?"

"You probably want my father. He's the new owner."

"Yes, that's right. May I speak to him?"

"He's not here right now. He went to see the manager to sign some papers."

"This is the manager speaking, and there are no papers to sign. He has to go to the garage to choose his parking space. Would you please let him know?"

I stare blankly at the telephone after I have hung up. What the hell? Why is my father lying to me? Will this week be the scene of more than a simple house move?

A memory comes to life. How old was I then? Fourteen? Yes, that's right. We had just celebrated my birthday and now we were going on vacation. My parents stopped on the highway to buy gas and drinks. I cannot remember why I was in a bad mood that day, but in any case, I decided to stay in the car. I moved across to the driver's seat and started playing with the dashboard controls – blinkers, windshield wipers, door locks, and so on – until, weary of sulking, I decided to catch up with my parents.

Fifteen minutes later, my father realized that I had locked the doors and left the keys in the ignition. A mechanic was called. In a voice trembling with rage, my father told me "I'm not going to give you a good hiding in public, but believe me, you will pay for this."

What lives in my memory now is not so much the beating with a belt that he gave me when we arrived at the rental villa, but the way in which his anger exploded after several hours on the road during which he had hummed along to the radio and regaled my mother with some racy jokes that the mechanic had told him. Barely had we put the suitcases down in the entrance hall than my father was calmly removing the belt from his pants and then, in an instant, his face was transformed. One second, he was calm and relaxed; the next, his features were deformed by a rage that he had guarded, pure and undiminished, inside him. I can see it quite clearly even now: it is not the pain of those blows that stayed with me, but the way my father carefully preserved his anger, ready to unleash it when the time came. I never looked at him in the same way after that day.

There is more. There is worse. Much worse! While I was leaning on the sink, my shorts around my ankles, the belt stinging my flesh, I had stared as if hypnotized at the pair of scissors close to me on the counter. The intensity of that moment has not been dimmed by time. I don't know what might have happened had my father not leaned over my shoulder and pushed those scissors out of my reach. Often, I think back to the temptation that had filled me then, and I wonder if my father had sensed that I was close to doing something irreparable.

The telephone rings again.

"Helloooo! Hello, Raoul!" The voice is a young man's. The way he prolonged that first "hello," his voice comically high-pitched, makes me think that this is his vocal signature, an effect reserved for people he knows well.

"Um, no, it's Philippe, his son."

No reaction. Not a word, not a sound.

"Hello?"

Another few seconds of silence and then I hear the dial tone. I have just hung up when I hear my father struggling to unlock the door. I open it for him.

"I hate these piece-of-shit magnetic cards!" he grumbles. "Give me an old-fashioned key any day."

"Everything go okay with the manager?"

I feel slightly ashamed at luring him into a trap like this. There is an echo of the questions he used to ask me when I came home from school, questions to which he already knew the answers. Perhaps this is the first skirmish in the battle to come.

He shrugs. "Just some paperwork to sign."

"The manager called, by the way. You're supposed to go down to the garage to choose your parking spot."

The look he shoots me before turning his back is brief, but as sharp as a razor blade.

"It's a shambles," is all he says. "I'll go there now."

I realize I have forgotten to mention the other mysterious phone call. Something tells me he would just shrug and change the subject.

The menu in the dining room did not tempt my father. "I have plenty of time to start eating my meals with these old farts," he declared, before adding that he did not like people his own age. "They're old."

"Maybe a place like this wasn't the best idea, then…"

"I couldn't live in our old apartment any longer. Too many memories. And I have no desire to move again in a few years, so I figured I may as well just skip to the next stage. Doesn't mean I have to like it."

On our way back to Paris, we eat dinner in a bistro very close to what I still think of as "home." The restaurant in question, Comme Chez Nous, has long been part of the neighborhood, but I cannot remember ever having gone there before.

The owner, who has the figure and face of a robust peasant woman, greets my father as if he is a regular.

"Is this your new local?" I ask, surprised.

"No, I still prefer Vittorio, but it's nice to vary things a little."

Pointing to the three words written at the top of the chalkboard advertising the day's specials, he adds "It's their stupid name that put me off for a long time. Comme Chez Nous! If I want to eat like I do at home, why would I bother going out at all?"

"But you changed your mind, apparently."

"When I was stuck on my own, eating frozen microwave meals, I decided to give them a chance. I figured it couldn't be any worse."

We sit facing each other, each of us sipping a glass of Kir – white wine flavored with blackcurrant liqueur.

"I thought you didn't drink anymore."

"True. But I'm eating dinner with my son."

Those words touch me. They also surprise me. The feelings that my father provokes in me are a collection of contradictions. I have often mentally compared us to two boxers dancing around the ring, each sizing up their opponent.

For a moment there is silence between us. My father stares at the bottom of his glass, then says "I'm happy for you that you're successful. You're making a good living, right?"

"For me, the success consists in doing what I love."

"And nobody could ever claim I encouraged you."

"Don't feel bad, Dad. All's well that ends well."

"I know, I know, but… you have to understand. The people who raised me couldn't have cared less about my education. They couldn't have cared less about me, in fact. All they wanted was the money."

"I know. You told me."

"I had no education, so I started as a waiter and later became a salesman. I was lucky that my boss paid me to take a management class in the evenings, but I never had many opportunities, really. Anyway, my point is that, when you used to tell me you wanted to work in the movies, it just seemed like a fantasy to me. Unrealistic."

But the movies were my passion. I started out as a gopher, before being eventually promoted to a second assistant, then first assistant on a short film. That job put me in constant dialog with the cinematographer, a position that I felt certain would one day be mine.

"How's everything at home?" my father asks. He never speaks Sophie's name. There was an awkwardness between them from their very first meeting, from which no one has been able to escape. It would be excessive to describe this situation as a cold war; perhaps a lukewarm stand-off would be more accurate.

I had never introduced any of my girlfriends to my parents before, but I knew I had met the woman I wanted to share my life with. At the time I was a first assistant, so I had to save up before I could book a table at Bofinger, my father's favorite brasserie. Sophie looked truly beautiful that night. She wore a pale-brown blazer, a pair of black jeans, and a cream blouse that set off her suntan – she had just returned from a week with Lucie at a friend's house in Sainte Maxime. I noticed people at other tables looking admiringly at her.

He was cheerful to begin with, but my father's mood deteriorated as he drank. He drank a lot back then. I had noticed my mother's worried glances as he kept draining his glass, as his tone became more strident. I had even attempted to ignore the empty bottle in the middle of the table, but had been help-less to prevent him enthusiastically approving the wine waiter's offer. "Yes, yes," he said. "Let's get another one. It's very nice, this Gigondas."

Turning to me, he had added defiantly "You don't have a problem with that, I hope?"

I sometimes tease Sophie by calling her a snob. It is not a snobbery based on money or class, but rather on a sharp sense of style and culture. Not that she did anything to show off that evening, but I quickly realized that she and my father lived on different planets. Loosened by alcohol and probably sensing that he had hit a nerve, he started to overdo it, ridiculing the worlds of fashion and the arts, contrasting what he called solid values like work, endurance, and courage with the pointless pastimes of lazy, good-for-nothing artists "who ought to get off their asses and pitch in with the rest of us instead."

We were waiting for the desserts to arrive when Sophie ex-cused herself. She had spotted a friend and wanted to go over and say hello.

When she had left the table, I turned to my parents, smil-ing as a way of inviting them to compliment me on my choice of partner. Instead, my father grumbled "She came in jeans. Your mother and I dressed up."

"What? Oh, Dad, come on! Jeans or not, she got dressed up for you too. What she's wearing is really chic, you know. And it really suits her."

"If that's what you like, good for you. And you never told us she's married."

"Was. She's in the process of getting a divorce."

"Still…."

"Still what?"

"Please, not here," my mother begged us. In vain, as usual.

"Still… I'd have preferred it if you settled down with a real young woman."

"What the hell does that mean, Dad? Do you even realize what you're saying?"

Sophie came back just then, and she saw the vexation on my face.

"Everything okay?" she asked, looking concerned. I reassured her with a nod.

"Sorry about that," she said to my parents. "Mylène is an old friend of mine. In fact, I lived with her for a month after I left Nate, my ex. Well, soon-to-be-ex. This divorce is taking forever!"

"Nate?" my father asked. "What kind of name is that?"

"His name is Nathan. He got used to being called Nate when he was at college in Boston."

"Nathan! Oh, so he's a--"

Like the soldier who leaps on top of the grenade as it is about to explode, I intervened "Yes, Dad, he's Jewish. He's a renowned radiologist."

But my father was not about to let go of his bone. "I'm just saying… your divorce is going to cost you."

"Dad!"

"What? Everyone knows what those people are like with money."

The silence on the way home lay heavy between us. Finally, Sophie gave a long sigh, and I said "You have no idea how sorry I am."

"You're the one I feel sorry for."

There was no second family dinner. Unwilling to risk another humiliation, I evaded my mother's occasional invitations with a range of excuses that ran from Sophie's professional obligations to vacations with her daughter to minor illnesses.

Sometimes, after spending the evening with my parents, I would mention to Sophie my mother's mood swings, her tendency to take refuge in a sad silence. She is so sweet and gentle, I would say, but so fragile.

"Your mom has a secret," Sophie said to me one day.

"What do you mean?"

"I don't know exactly, but I bet you anything she's hiding behind a secret."

"What makes you say that?"

"It's just an impression. I only saw her once – that awful night – but there was something in her look. I remember thinking, that woman is hiding something. Something important."

"Philippe!" my father says.

"What?"

"I asked if everything is all right at home."

"Oh, sorry, Dad. Yes, everything's fine. I spend too much time traveling, but I'm always very happy to get home once it's over."

He nods, then starts eating his onion soup. That is the end of that conversation.

Back when I used to meet my mother to eat lunch near the hospital where she worked, she would question me about my future. "Are you going to marry her?" she often asked.

I replied that Sophie and I saw no need to get married.

"What if you have children?"

"Sophie already has a daughter. I love Lucie like she's my own, and I already feel guilty about being absent so often. If we had a baby together, I wouldn't even get to watch it grow up."

I never told her that Sophie and I have been separated twice. Those setbacks in our relationship have left us cautious. At the same time, overcoming them has given us enough faith in our union not to need the official seal of a ceremony.

My thoughts return to my father, who has never mastered the art of eating soup without making a noise. I imagine him in the dining room at Résidence Bellevue.

He looks up and catches me looking at him.

"What?"

"Why do you keep saying 'what'?"

"What were you thinking about?"

"Nothing important. I just still can't understand why you chose that retirement home."

He stiffens, then shrugs. "I already told you. What more do you want?"

"I don't know," I sigh. "The image I have of you is of someone who weighs up the pros and cons, who always finds the perfect bargain, and this…that place is a long way from anything. The only thing you can find to recommend it is the restaurant, and you don't even want to eat there. I'm just trying to get my head round it."

His eyes shrink back and the look in them becomes cold, almost hostile. His tone, when he replies to me, puts an end to what had seemed like the start of a new era between us – or a truce, at least.

"I'm not accountable to you," he says, abruptly terminating the conversation.

We finish the meal in silence. When the waiter brings us the check and I pick it up, my father makes not the slightest sign of protest, nor does he utter a single word of thanks.

Chapter Three

I struggle awake, staring in confusion before I accept the reality of the decor of a room that was mine for so many years; today, it is both familiar and very strange. On thousands of mornings in the past, I would open my eyes and see those curtains, through which I could guess at the weather that awaited me on my walk to school. Now I am a visitor.

I find my father fully dressed in the kitchen. He is reading his *Le Parisien* newspaper. A magnifying glass with an ivory handle is on the table beside him. Catching sight of me through his glasses – one branch of which is wrapped in a Band-Aid – he stubs out his cigarette in a saucer. I hesitate to move toward him, but he smiles at me and offers me his unshaved cheek.

"Did you sleep well?"

So, all is forgotten, apparently.

"Yes, thanks. What's with the magnifying glass?"

"For the small print. My eyesight, you know…"

"You should get new glasses."

He shrugs.

"They cost a fortune. Anyway, I get tired of fighting this

rearguard action against old age all the time. I don't want to get you down, but you'll see what I mean one day."

This is my father's idea of humor. I try changing the subject.

"Do you still read the sports page first?"

He shakes his head. "Not anymore. These days, I start with the obituaries. Looking out for names I recognize. I look at the ages too, you know, to get a sense of where I stand. You probably think that's pathetic."

"Not at all. I imagine that I'll be the same, one day, like you said…" My voice trails off momentarily, but I conclude "I didn't realize that you were so preoccupied with death."

Another shrug, accompanied by a mirthless laugh.

"It's part of my daily life now. Knowing that I'm getting close to the end has colored the way I see lots of things. For example, I saw a nice coat last week in a store window, and mine is pretty tatty. I was about to go into the store when I thought, how many times a year will I even wear that coat – for funerals, mostly – and how many years do I have left? So I just kept walking. My sheepskin jacket is perfectly fine. You see what I mean?" My father puts down the newspaper and points to a paper bag on the table. "Anyway, that's enough of all that! I went out to get you a pain au chocolat. See? I haven't forgotten."

Gesturing with his chin at the Cona coffee-maker, he adds "And I made us some coffee. Very strong – the way you like it. You can pour us some if you like."

"Thanks, Dad. That's great."

I won't tell him that I prefer tea in the mornings now, with porridge or cereal.

As I gaze at the background to my adolescence, I try to imagine myself here as a teenage boy, but find it hard to conjure such a vision. And yet nothing has really changed, apart from a few minor details like the flower-patterned curtain in front of the window overlooking the courtyard, a new microwave, and, of course, the collection of spice jars that I brought my parents once from a shoot in an exotic location. The past resists my efforts to re-enter it; the border is closed, for now.

Smoothing the front page of the newspaper with his hand, my father says "I'll miss that young Le Pen girl – Marine's niece. She had a gift for politics. It's a shame she's giving it up. And boy, was she cute!"

I nod, in silence. I made a resolution and I am going to stick to it: no politics. The few conversations we have had on the subject over the years have convinced me that we are never going to agree on anything. For my father, I am a soft-hearted liberal, an advocate of gay marriage, mosques on the corner of every street, borders wide open to every foreigner who wants to come here and take advantage of our social welfare system, blah blah blah. As for him, I would be willing to bet that he voted for the quasi-fascist Front National. We have nothing to gain – and everything to lose – by squaring up over this, and there is zero chance of either of us persuading the other to change his mind.

"Don't you think she's cute?"

"Sure. You want sweetener in your coffee?"

"She has ideas too, though. That's why it's a shame she's given up."

"Yes, Dad."

"What's that supposed to mean – 'Yes, Dad'?"

"What should I have said? 'No, Dad'?"

"It's your tone of voice. And that smile – what's that supposed to mean?"

"Nothing, except that you remind me of a matador, waving his red flag. You're trying to pick a fight so you can deliver the death blow."

"Oh really? Well, if that's how you're going to take it, let's just drop the subject!"

I watch the way he lifts his bowl of coffee to his nose and breathes in its aroma, frowning.

"Something wrong?" I ask.

He puts down the bowl. "Let me explain… the smell of coffee always used to get me out of bed. Your mom would be up before me. I would fill my nostrils with that scent and it was one of the best moments of my day. But ever since my operation, I've lost all sense of smell. I know it doesn't sound like much – anyone can live without it – but you'd be amazed how much I miss it. So, you see, even though I know I can't smell anything, I can't help sniffing my coffee in the morning, in the hope that it will come back."

He chuckles and winks at me. "But there are good sides to this too. I can't smell the caretaker's cooking anymore!" Now he laughs openly. "There was a vote at the last owners' meeting; were we going to invest in a ventilation system to get rid of those smells? I voted against the motion, just to piss them off. One of the *folles* on the third floor started raving at me 'But Monsieur Lamont, doesn't it bother you, the awful stench of that woman's food?' Yeah, 'awful stench' – that's what he actually said. I mean, it's what *she* actually said. I acted all innocent and tolerant. I even said something like different cultures, different cuisines, we have to be understanding…"

My father, the champion of tolerance! The defender of

43

immigrants! This man who always lumps together Arabs, Jews, blacks, homos, and refugees as undesirables.

We slowly eat breakfast together, occasionally making brief comments about the headlines in the newspaper, which we have divided up.

"I'm going to clear the table and then check my emails," I say, getting to my feet.

"Just stay a bit longer."

I recognize the face he wears when he is about to announce something important, that way he has of sitting up tall and moistening his lips with the tip of his tongue.

"I was thinking," he begins.

"Uh-oh!"

"Yes, all right, very funny. But seriously, Philippe, we're going to fill boxes for the Salvation Army. I'm going to go through the bookshelves, and you, if this doesn't sound too boring…"

His words trail off.

"Yes?"

"I'd like it if you could take care of your mom's things. Her dresses, her trinkets, her shoes. Well, all of it."

He notices the lack of enthusiasm on my face.

"I have to admit," he says, "it's hard for me."

Whereas I was completely unaffected by my mother's death, I suppose? I am about to protest, but I manage to control myself. I have to be understanding. The suicide of his wife after nearly fifty years together must have left a hole in his life that is impossible to fill. Whereas for me, as painful and disorienting as the news was, I was lucky to have the preoccupations of my career. I also got back together with Sophie.

"Well, someone has to do it," I say at last.

"Thank you, Philippe. I'll leave you in charge of that, then?"

———— ⚬⚬⚬ ————

In the bedroom that my parents used to share, I sit on the bed, granting myself a moment of grace before I confront the remnants of the past. Looking back, for me, is above all an exercise in remembering missed opportunities, bad choices, lost loves, failures, the pain I have caused others. I am aware that there have also been successes, happy surprises, moments of pleasure and joy, but they have left little trace in my memory. I wish I could change my nature, but the truth is that I lack the serenity necessary to be happy. Sophie, who understands me so well, is patiently helping me to find peace. Better late than never.

I reach out toward the framed photograph that has always sat on their nightstand. My father has not touched it. The picture shows me sitting to my mother's right. Her hand lies on top of mine. I must have been about fifteen. She looks so young, so beautiful! In fact, she stayed beautiful until the end. The gray hair that she never bothered dyeing and the lines around her eyes and mouth never overshadowed the light that shone from her pale green eyes. Ever since childhood, I used to think that my mother was the most beautiful woman in the world, but did I ever take the time to judge her objectively, to realize that she genuinely was an exceptionally beautiful woman?

With my fingernail, I trace the shape of her nose, her lips (rarely covered in lipstick), her chin. As part of my job, I often rub shoulders with models, starlets and famous actresses, and I think I have an eye for beauty. And in all honesty, my mother would not have looked out of place in that world. My fingertip lingers on the arc-shaped scar, like a close bracket symbol, partially invisible behind a lock of blonde hair. It runs – or rather, it ran – from her left temple to the top of her cheekbone. My mother never bothered concealing it with make-up. That was not her style.

She often told me the story of her accident. She was eight years old and she was running around the swimming pool behind the family mansion, dressed in a brand-new bathing suit, when she slid on the slippery tiles and fell, headfirst, into the lifeguard's high chair. The lifeguard jumped down and carried her in his arms. "I didn't cry," she said. "But my face was covered with blood." Her father fired the lifeguard, who had failed to carry out his order to pad the legs of his chair.

It is time now. I stand for a moment in front of the chest of drawers that contain my mother's underwear. Gathering my courage, I open the three drawers and grab handfuls of panties, bras, and tights. To think how I used to explore these secret spaces when I was a boy, heart pounding. How mysterious it all seemed back then!

My mother caught me one day, rubbing a pair of her white knickers against my cheek.

"What are you doing?" she asked. "Are you looking for something? It's not something you should ever do, you know, going through other people's belongings."

"I know, Mom. But it's so soft."

My mother closed the drawer and sat me down next to her on the big bed. Once again, she told me about her golden childhood.

"Yes, that underwear is soft, but in reality, it's just nylon.

When I was young, I wore only silk. Layla, one of my maids – she was Moroccan, a lovely woman – used to wash all my things by hand. Then she would iron them and scent them with perfumes from her country. The other maids were not allowed into my room. Well, except for the cleaning ladies, obviously."

"How many servants did your family have?"

"You always ask the same question, but I've told you, I don't remember. With the chauffeur, the cooks, the two gardeners, the maids…I just never counted, you know!"

"And here, we have a cleaning lady who comes once a week."

"That's true, my Philou, but I also have your Daddy and my sweet little boy."

If I knew my mother's maiden name, I would be able to Google her rich parents, but I never thought to ask when I was a child and all such questions, in later years, went unanswered. My parents always refused to revisit the past; both of them said they preferred to forget the old days, to focus on the present. So they would not even tell me her previous surname, an attitude that always struck me as excessive, even if I never gave it that much thought. I was not particularly upset about not knowing my maternal grandparents.

Mechanically, I fill two trash bags. I act as if I am accomplishing a task that has nothing to do with me.

Now I turn to the wardrobe, with its hanging dresses, skirts, and pants. Two pale blue nurses' uniforms, too. I wish I could believe that she might reappear at any moment. I am standing there, arms dangling, before those clothes, wondering if they remind me of her life or of her death, when I hear my father discreetly cough behind me. He has brought me a cup of coffee.

"Thank you, Philippe," he says before leaving. "I know it's not easy."

I pull up a chair and drink my coffee. My God, it's strong – I'm not used to it anymore. Memories of other stories my mother told me come to mind. Her parents were violently opposed to her marriage with a "penniless nobody." They tried blackmailing her, threatened to disinherit her – which they did – and promised her a cruise around the world if she agreed to listen to reason. But my mother did not give in; she married the man she loved. And she never regretted it, she often told me. My parents were married in the town hall in Nice, with two of my father's colleagues as witnesses. The four of them then ate dinner together in a restaurant in the old town. "I never heard from my parents again," she concluded. "You see, Philippe, everyone has to make choices in life. For me, it was a choice between wealth, comfort and luxury, or love. What do you think is most important?"

I lift the coat hangers off the rail and pile all these clothes on the bed before cramming them into three cardboard boxes. I will need another one for the women's magazines and medical reviews stacked in the bottom drawer.

At the last moment, I take out one of my mother's favorite dresses and carry it to my bedroom in a desperate attempt to save the past from obliteration.

For lunch, there are oeufs à la russe and a vegetable julienne. "I know the guy who runs the caterer round the corner," my father explains. "Have you finished in the bedroom yet?"

"No, I still have to do the cupboard, but I needed to take a break. No matter how hard you try not to think about it, just do your job, the memories are waiting there to ambush you. You recognize a skirt, a blouse, a scarf, and suddenly you're back there with her. So that's enough for today."

"I know, Philippe, I know. That's why I keep thanking you."

We have just sat down when my cell phone vibrates. I read the text, then sigh with exasperation. "These producers are driving me crazy. This is the third time they've asked me to review my budget. They claim they can't afford to pay the star unless they make cuts elsewhere."

"But you're a partner. You have a say in this, don't you?"

"Actually, my status is ambiguous – I'm a freelance cinematographer, but also a partner – and that's making things difficult. As the movie's cinematographer, I just want to send them packing. As a partner, I want to make this movie with Charlize Theron."

"Charlize Theron! That's the hot blonde, right?"

"And an excellent actress, too. I'm going to tell them they have to economize somewhere else. If I lose any more of my budget, they may as well use a camcorder. Let's see what Charlize Theron thinks about that…"

"You're a lucky guy," my father says, "hanging around with all those beautiful women."

"Oh, you know…."

"I bet you don't get bored on shoots. You must have plenty of opportunities."

This conversation is making me a little uneasy. My father and I have never confided in each other.

I am no Casanova, but I couldn't claim to be a saint, either. It's true that the weeks spent shooting a movie are conducive to affairs. Actors, actresses, everyone from the script girl to the cameraman is living together on another planet for weeks, sometimes even months. Far from our friends and partners, we travel together, stay in the same hotels, eat at the same tables, work day and night, and hang out together when the work is over and we want to relax. It's hardly a surprise that what my favorite cameraman Jacky calls "oopsies" should be covered by a blanket absolution that is both tacit and collective. What happens on a shoot never happened, as they say.

Few of these affairs survive beyond the shoot. Whether you have slept together or not, you say goodbye at the airport baggage claim, wish each other good luck and promise to stay in touch, knowing perfectly well that this is all a performance. And when you meet again months later at the movie's premiere, you kiss each other on the cheek with barely a thought for those other, more intimate kisses you have shared in the past.

There are exceptions to this rule, though, and I once made the mistake of letting a shoot romance linger on after our return to Paris. Marlène, a make-up artist with an infectious laugh and a body that could stop traffic, stroked my leg with her bare foot one night under the dinner table and, later that night, joined me in my room. The shoot, in Morocco, was coming to an end, and the wisest decision would have been to accept that it was nothing but a wonderful memory, but then there were two weeks in a studio in Boulogne, and we continued our lovemaking. Everything was different in Paris, because Sophie was waiting for me at home and Marlène was married to a man who ran a bar. So we started meeting in hotel rooms, and I discovered a taste for – and the bitter aftertaste of – adultery. I was preparing to retake control of my life when Marlène's husband, having paid a detective to trail her, sent Sophie a photograph showing his wife standing next to me in the doorway of a hotel in Porte Maillot. That evening, Sophie packed her bags. "For a few weeks on a shoot," she said, "well… I don't like it, but I can turn a blind eye. But not here, where we live. It's over."

It took me more than a year to win her back by convincing her that I had learned my lesson.

"So?" my father insists. "Any pretty actresses?"

I shake my head and respond with a question of my own "What about you? Any pretty saleswomen?"

"You're crazy. Never, you hear me? Anyway…pretty? Only after a few drinks."

My father is not aware that, one day, when I was thirteen, as I was tired of waiting for him in the parking lot after he'd gone back to the store because he had "forgotten something," I went off to find him. That was how I came to see him through the blinds at the window of his office, sharing an interminable kiss with Josette, the red-headed cashier. I ran back to the car as fast as my legs would carry me. I remember telling my parents that I wasn't feeling well that evening, and going to bed without eating dinner. There was no moral aspect to my distress, not at all; the emotion that filled me was simply fear. I had the feeling that the kiss I had witnessed was the herald of some terrible misfortune, an earthquake that might easily destroy my little world.

"So you never… not even once?"

He glares at me. "Never. What the hell is with all these questions?"

"I'm sorry, Dad, but you started it."

"Well… all right then. Let's just drop the subject."

Just as well, I think. I do not judge him for his misdemeanor – or misdemeanors, perhaps – and I do not doubt that he loved his wife, but a voice in the back of my head regrets that this first attempt at camaraderie between father and son should end with a lie. Although…be honest, Philippe, wouldn't you have lied in his place?

As I shrug, my father starts telling me the plan for the afternoon.

I hesitate for several minutes before entering the cellar. All it would take is the slightest misstep and I could cause an avalanche of boxes and bags that would literally bury me under years of memories.

Starting with the summit of this precarious mountain of stuff, I put several of the cardboard boxes in the hallway and begin a basic inventory. This one contains some faded green curtains that I vaguely remember, the next a frayed bathrobe and a collection of old towels. The third contains shirts, shorts, and sweaters from my childhood; the fourth a single rubber boot and some moth-eaten scarves. I laugh inwardly – who would keep a single boot? – and then start going through some plastic supermarket bags, dust cloths, mismatched gloves, old socks.

The clothes that are still wearable will go to the Salvation Army while the other useless relics will be stuffed in trash bags and put out for the garbage collectors. Lastly, there are certain objects whose fate can be decided only by my father. "I'm ready to let go of it all," he has assured me.

One last box, I tell myself, and then I'll be ready for a good shower.

It is a cardboard crate with the Kronenbourg logo on the side and its contents leave me puzzled: a pair of boxing gloves, two pairs of shorts, a jump rope, two towels, and a leather head-protector of a sort that I remember seeing once when I was working on a documentary about the romance between Edith Piaf and the world champion boxer Marcel Cerdan. Never had my father ever mentioned being a boxer. And what about this thing, underneath – a stick full of nails, on a strap. What could that be? Ah, and this, right at the bottom, wrapped up in a dirty cloth? A metal object with four holes. I frown before realizing that I am holding brass knuckles, just like the ones that we used for gangster movies.

I spent the rest of the afternoon in a bathrobe on my bed, talking to the director, who was not at all happy about the proposed budget cuts. I listened patiently as he compared himself to Tarantino, and then I also talked to Jacky, the cameraman, who told me he was leaving for Toronto in two days; a feature film with a Canadian crew.

"So, you see, I'm doing fine," he told me. "And if you do the camera work yourself, you'll have your savings."

He also offered me his two invitations to the premiere of a movie called *Tapis Roulant*, a second film by one of his friends. "It's tomorrow," he explained. "I'll be busy packing. I'll send you a link – you just have to print the tickets."

After that, I called Sophie, who persists in asking me if am "still being a good boy for your daddy." She can't resist twisting the knife once it's lodged in my flesh. I have no choice but to wait for her to grow weary of this joke. Yes, I told her, everything is going as planned. The week is just getting started.

And now, my father pokes his head through my doorway. "Why don't we go to eat dinner at Vittorio, the best pizzeria in Paris?" he suggests. "I haven't been back there for ages."

The owner has not forgotten him, however.

"Signor Lamont!' he exclaims. 'What a pleasure to see you again, and how is…."

He suddenly stops speaking, eyes widened, interrupted in mid-flow, I suspect, by the dark look that my father must have flashed at him. My father is standing next to me, so I can't see his face, but I sense his whole body tense. Vittorio quickly recovers his composure. "I'm so sorry, I was thinking about something else…"

Grabbing hold of my hand, he hurriedly adds "If I remember correctly, you are the son. You haven't changed much! But I'm sorry, I cannot recall your name."

"Philippe."

We shake hands and Vittorio leads us to our table.

"A cold San Pellegrino, Mr. Lamont?"

"No, Vittorio. Bring us a bottle of Chianti. A good vintage."

"A half-bottle?"

"A bottle. I am spending the week with my son. I can go back to being reasonable next week."

After the antipasti, a silence falls between us as we wait for our Four Seasons pizza to arrive.

"An angel passing," my father says, the old cliché to explain an awkward silence. Then he adds "Strange, isn't it, this obligation we always feel to keep talking? Personally, I don't feel any need to maintain a conversation all the time."

"You don't say, Dad!" I say, winking at him.

Tonight, I'm silent because I can't stop thinking about the discovery I made that afternoon, yet I do not know how to bring up the subject. Once again, I am irritated to realize just how much my father still intimidates me.

I fill our glasses and swallow a mouthful. *Come on*, I cajole myself. *No time like the present...*

"Were you into sports when you were young, Dad?"

"A little bit. I played soccer, but mainly just so I could hang out with my friends. I used to swim, too, when I had access to a pool."

"And apart from that?"

"What do you mean?"

'I don't know... any other sports?'

"No, not really. What are you getting at?"

"Oh, it's no big deal. Just one of the boxes I found in the cellar. There was a pair of boxing gloves inside, and some shorts and a jump rope...you know, like boxers use when they're training. I was just wondering."

He shakes his head. "No idea."

An instinct for caution holds me back from mentioning the studded club and the knuckledusters.

"A couple of times, I helped out friends who were between apartments," he says. "They would sometimes leave their things at our place for a month or two. One of them probably forgot it there."

"Sure, Dad, that makes sense. I was just wondering, that's all."

The pizza arrives, cut into six slices, and Vittorio comes over to make sure we are satisfied. As he jokes with my father, I think about the stack of flyers I found at the bottom of that box. The name of Raoul Lamont featured on the program for the junior championships of the Georges Carpentier boxing club in Clermont-Ferrand, and the sepia photograph of my father was one of four that illustrated the facing page. I know nothing about the age categories of boxing, but in that photo he looked about eighteen or nineteen years old.

———— ◊◊◊ ————

The elevator is stuck between floors. "They really need to replace this piece of junk someday," my father says, "but they'll have to do it without me."

With a gesture, he invites me to go first and we begin climbing the coarsely carpeted stairs. As I stop on the fourth floor to turn the light back on (it is on a timer and has just plunged us into darkness), I realize my father is nowhere to be seen. I lean over the balustrade and call out "Dad?"

There is a long silence, and then I hear a weak, breathless voice say "I'm here. I'm okay. Give me a minute."

I find him sitting on the lowest step of the second landing, his elbows resting on his knees, head between his hands. I sit next to him. "What's wrong, Dad?"

"Nothing, really. Just a bit out of breath. That damn elevator!"

I take out a handkerchief and wipe the sweat from his forehead.

"Take your time, Dad. There's no rush."

I realize that time has taken its toll on my father without me noticing. My parents watched me grow up, but I didn't really see them grow old. I have seen very little of my father since my mother's funeral; we have mostly just talked on the phone. As strange as it sounds, the image of him in my head has barely changed since I left home more than twenty-five years ago. Of course, I noticed when his hair turned white, then disappeared, when his back started to bend and his movements became a little hesitant. I also accepted his decision to live in a retirement community, but this confrontation with the reality of his decline catches me off guard. The abstract has given way to the concrete. I know that my father is an old man now, even if he is not yet an invalid. Seeing him exhausted after climbing two flights of stairs gives me a sudden grasp of the destructive power of the passing years. For me, it's the equivalent of a close-up. I am deeply moved.

"To think I used to take these steps two at a time," he sighs.

"Smoking like a chimney doesn't exactly help. You must know that."

"I don't want to give up all my pleasures."

Formidable, dictatorial, violent, self-assured…the father of the little boy I used to be occupies a special place in my life. Sometimes I have the impression that I have turned him into a statue, a symbol of indestructability. Up there on his pedestal, he represents authority and vigor. I am finding it hard to come to terms with the idea that his strength is abandoning him.

One hand gripping the balustrade, my father pulls himself to his feet. He pats my shoulder with his other hand Come on, let's go," he says. But slowly, all right?"

When I knock at his bedroom door later that evening, I find him under the covers. Leaning against two piled-up pillows, he is watching television with the sound off.

"How do you feel?"

He smiles and shrugs in an attempt to reassure me. "I'll be okay. That'll teach me to try to climb the stairs as fast as you. Don't worry, just go to bed."

"Do you want me to turn the volume up?"

"Nah, don't bother. I just daydream when it's on. That's how I fall asleep when I'm alone. I'll turn it off when I get up to piss."

I do not close the door when I leave his room. When I was a kid and he used to tuck me in at night, I would always remind him to leave my door open and the lamp in the corridor on.

Chapter Four

As I awake, I instinctively reach out to my right, as I do every morning, to touch Sophie's shoulder or her hip. Her presence is a stabilizing factor in my life.

When people ask how we met, I warn them that they probably won't believe me.

After being promoted for the first time, I stopped sleeping on the couch of an electrician friend and began to share the double bed belonging to Josh Adams, another colleague, who worked as a stunt driver. His girlfriend had just left him for a painter, and the two of us were rarely in Paris at the same time.

Josh lived on Allée des Plantes, an enclave of the twentieth arrondissement that opened onto Rue des Pyrénées, very close to the Père Lachaise cemetery. With its first-floor studio apartments on either side of the narrow alley, this private residence looked as if it had once housed a stable.

Josh had invited a few friends to a New Year's Eve party he was hosting and we had gone shopping during the day. In the evening I went out again to buy three bottles of cheap champagne at Monoprix. It was almost 10:00 when I arrived outside the door at Allée des Plantes, where Sophie was struggling with the security code. She was carrying a bag bearing the logo of Nicolas, the wine store.

We knew each other by sight. I had of course noticed the natural elegance of this slim, young blonde woman, whom I imagined to be a fashion model. I would have loved to get to know her better but – I may as well admit it – she intimidated me.

"Can I help you?" I asked.

"They keep changing the code. If you hold this, I can look for the new one in my handbag."

The door was quickly opened and we had just wished each other a Happy New Year when I heard Sophie hiss "God damn it!"

I turned around. "What's the matter?"

She looked simultaneously annoyed and amused. As I would discover, Sophie has a gift for seeing the absurdity in any difficult situation.

"It's ridiculous," she said, collapsing onto one of the stone benches that decorated the alley. My first thought was that she must have lost her keys.

The reality was a little weirder. A few days earlier, the occupants of the studio across the street, knowing that she was alone, had invited her to spend New Year's Eve with them.

"We're not friends," she explained, "but we say hello and do each other small favors occasionally. I have nothing against them, but I also had no desire to celebrate the New Year with them. They're just…boring! You know, they're the sort of people who see the best in everyone. It's like living in Disneyland or something!"

So Sophie had turned down their invitation, using the first excuse that came to mind: she had already been invited somewhere else.

"Ah, that's a shame," the neighbor said. "Where are you going?"

"Um…a friend's house…in the suburbs."

She had given the matter no further thought. As she always did for New Year's Eve, she had ordered a feast for herself: a dozen oysters, foie gras, a capon with morel mushrooms, and a selection of sorbets. She had gone out just now to buy a half-bottle of Dom Pérignon.

"The full works, you know!" she said.

"So?"

"So I bumped into my neighbor earlier and she said she hoped I would have a lovely time with my friend in the suburbs. And now it's just hit me; if I go home and turn on the lights, they'll know that I lied to them. Their window is right opposite mine."

I leapt at this chance to rescue her "I live with a friend over there, on the ground floor. Why don't you come to our place? Your neighbors will never see you."

She shook her head. "Thank you, but I'm afraid I have a character flaw: once I've got an idea in my head, I simply have to go through with it. I can already taste those oysters. Still, it is going to be a little bizarre, sad in fact, celebrating in the dark…"

"Unless…."

"Unless?"

I don't know where I got the nerve to ask her to celebrate the New Year with me in total darkness. She stared at me steadily for several seconds before observing "Well, you don't look like a rapist."

"Careful! Angelic looks can be deceiving."

"I didn't say you looked angelic."

That was all it took. We both smiled, knowing already that we liked each other.

A few hours later, I was not lying when I told Josh that I had just enjoyed the best New Year's Eve of my life. The meal, intended for one person, had been fairly meager, but the abundance of champagne more than compensated for that, and we had talked and talked all evening. The darkness turned us, strangers just moments before, into confidantes revealing in hushed voices intimate thoughts we would never have shared in more conventional circumstances. I told her about my struggle to live with the scars of a rough childhood and my efforts to be a better man than my father had been. She shared memories of her failed marriage.

Brought up in stifling bourgeois comfort in Lyon, Sophie's ambition to one day be a painter had provoked outrage in her strict and austere parents. She couldn't be serious! The law was what she needed to study. Later she would meet the "right" kind of husband.

When she met a young Parisian radiologist, who was in Lyon for a convention, her whole life changed. Four days of passion had been followed by three months of daily phone calls, and when he asked her to marry him, she had jumped at the opportunity. Her parents offered only token resistance to the marriage, the benefits of social prestige trumping any qualms they had about their daughter marrying a Jew.

"Paris was everything I dreamed it would be. Of course, I was in love with Nate, but with hindsight I can see that what I really fell for was freedom."

Over time, Doctor Jekyll transformed into Mister Hyde.

A serial adulterer with a jealous streak, Nate began to suspect that his wife's life was just as dissolute as his own. He became a control freak, demanding that she provide him with a precise account of how she spent every hour of every day. As a way to keep her under his control, he scoffed at her artistic ambitions and denigrated her talent. Finally, he forbade her to paint at home and banished her easel, palette, tubes of paint, and all vestiges of her equipment from their apartment. "I can't stand having this mess around me," he would say. "You're wasting your time, anyway."

One day, she left this prison behind, moved into a renovated studio apartment Allée des Plantes where she started to work seriously on her painting, and joined forces with a friend who needed help decorating show homes. "It pays the rent," she said. "My only problem is dealing with the tastes of some of my clients. I'm not the most tolerant person in the world."

"What are your paintings about?" I asked.

"I work from vintage photographs of old family albums. I try to give them a whimsical touch."

"I'd love to see them."

She laughed. "They're all around us, but tonight is not a good time to see them."

"I'll have to come back, then."

A little girl was the only remaining link between Sophie and her husband. As Sophie waited for the divorce to be finalized, the two adults came to an agreement for sharing custody.

"I had her for Christmas, so she's with her father for the New Year."

Sophie was as mad about the movies as I was – everything

except science fiction and horror – and we discussed this mutual passion at length. I told her about my job, opting for tales about blunders, hysterical giggling fits in the middle of dramatic scenes, and other accidents of film-making rather than gossip about the stars. When one of us would laugh too loud, the other would shush. "The neighbors, remember!"

Sophie told me her age, without any false modesty. Although she was only two years older than me, she seemed infinitely more mature. She embodied the stability that I too often lacked.

"So how was it, your first time in the dark?" Josh asked as I helped him to tidy up at four in the morning.

"What do you mean?"

"Don't tell me you didn't take advantage of the situation!"

"We kissed on the cheeks at midnight."

"That's all?"

"No, not really. We're going for a walk in the Belleville park this afternoon."

What I did not tell him was that I felt certain I had met the woman of my dreams.

The elevator is still out of order, so I go out to do the shopping. The baker, a bald, corpulent man whom I vaguely recognize, cries out "Why, it's young Lamont!"

"Well, not as young as all that, Monsieur... um?"

"Ferrande."

"Of course. You have an impressive memory, Monsieur Ferrande. I've certainly changed quite a bit since my mother used to send me out to buy bread."

"You still have the same look in your eyes. Are you here to see your dad?"

"Yes, I'm spending the week with him."

"He must be happy. He's so proud of you. You should hear him talking about his son the cinematographer, fought over by all the studios!"

I am flabbergasted by this. If only he had told me.

Handing me a baguette – plus two croissants that I did not order – Ferrande says in a low voice "On the house. For you to share with your dad."

He wipes the flour off his hand before shaking mine.

"I was so sorry to hear about your mom. I hope they can find a cure for that damned disease."

So, my father must have told him a lie. I understand. I, too, am ashamed of the truth, as if he and I were to blame somehow.

"They taste even better when they're free," my father declares, dunking his croissant in his bowl of coffee. He's also busy sorting through the mail I have just brought him.

"Another one!" he exclaims, waving a black-edged envelope. "They're dropping like flies these days."

He reads the announcement, sighs, then explains "It's Jean-Marc. He was one of the witnesses at our wedding. You remember when he came to spend a week here?"

"Vaguely. It didn't end well, if I recall correctly."

"True. He thought it was funny to call us Mr. and Mrs. Scarface. I told him not to start with that, but he made the same joke in front of some friends of ours. As soon as the guests had left, I threw him out on the landing with his suitcase. We never spoke after that. I knew he'd have to die before I ever heard from him again."

I have the uncomfortable feeling that some important information has just been shared without my paying it the attention it deserves. I try vainly to go back in time, to press the rewind button on my memory. For that, I need calm.

"I have some phone calls to make," I say, leaving the kitchen.

I lie on my bed for a while before a ray of light finally pierces the darkness. Yes, that's it: Mr. and Mrs. Scarface. Let me see...I remember clearly my mother's account of how she got her scar – falling into the lifeguard's chair – but that is not what I am searching for. I need to think about my father, about his scar. He had an accident when he was a little boy. He and a friend were playing at being circus knife-throwers. Okay... so? I feel as if there is a fly trapped inside my skull. I have to be patient; sooner or later, it will come to me. Well, I hope it will.

At last, I have an idea. I stand up and look inside my bag for the boxing tournament flyers that I found in the cellar. The photograph of my father is far from perfect, but one thing is clear: he does not have that scar. His face is posed three-quarters to the camera and his left cheek is in the foreground. He must have been in his late teens at the time, and there was no Photoshop back then. So, he must have gotten his scar later. Something is off, but what?

———— ∞ ————

"I sent a note offering my condolences to his son," my father says, before licking the seal of an envelope.

Now he copies down the address from the announcement and adds "I am not afraid of death. Really, I'm not. It's the journey there that I hate. I've had my whole life to get ready for old age – it's not like I'm the first person it's happened to – and yet, stupid as it sounds, it's taking me by surprise. I don't know how to deal with it. You see what I mean?"

"Not really."

"Take the other day, for example. I bumped into Mazurel. You remember him?"

"I don't think so."

"The chief accountant. He had a mustache and a clubfoot. He took his retirement before I did. We had a drink together and I asked him what he was up to. Afterward, I regretted asking him the question, because I couldn't find a way to shut him up. Get this: he's started collecting stamps. He's in a club of... what do you call them again?"

"Philatelists?"

"That's it! They sell or swap rare stamps. They even go abroad for special stamp fairs. At one point he took an envelope out of his wallet and showed me this Dutch stamp. I could look, but I couldn't touch. You should have heard him telling me the story of this stamp, how he found it and whatnot. And I listened to all this, and I could see this light in his eyes. I couldn't have cared less about his stamp, but I said to myself, he's lucky, Mazurel. He has a passion. That changes everything, at our age. But what am I passionate about?"

"You're interested in history."

"An interest isn't the same thing. It's not enough to get you out of bed in the morning. And anyway, why should I really care about the Treaty of Versailles?"

"But--"

He holds up his hand to cut me off. For some reason, he

has become suddenly open, voluble, as if a door inside his mind has been unbolted.

"What I lack are real desires. I remember when I was young I used to have ambitions, cravings, sudden enthusiasms. I took part in more than my share of stupid acts and I often regretted it afterward, but I felt alive. Nowadays, I feel like I'm carefully managing the years remaining to me."

"It's funny, Dad, hearing you talk about stupid acts and enthusiasms. That's not the image I have of you at all. For me, you were Monsieur Discipline, always so serious and severe. The kind of guy who always uses the crosswalk and counts his change."

"Nobody tells their children everything."

His words, not mine.

He sticks a stamp on the envelope, then stares into space for a moment. "It's true, I'm managing my time now. That's not living!"

I am not used to this aspect of my father. I feel as if I am listening to a stranger.

"All the same, Dad, you're doing really well on the whole. You're in really good physical shape for your age. You'll be one of the youngest and strongest in your new home."

The way he frowns now is more familiar to me.

"Yeah. I'll be able to look around me and contemplate my own future."

He gives a sort of sad snigger.

"You know, my son, I'm not trying to get you down, but if life was a meal, I'd send the dessert back. It doesn't taste very sweet, believe me."

I stand up so I can clear the table, and put a hand on his shoulder.

"In my job, everyone says it's just a question of lighting. Maybe it's time to turn on a few spotlights. Come on, I know something that might cheer you up. I've got two invitations to a premiere tonight. Do you want to come with me?"

"What movie is it?"

"A small, independent film. A comedy. It should be fun."

He stands up and shakes himself like a wet dog. "Sure, it'll make a change. Brooding isn't good for your health."

We park the car in the parking garage near the George V metro station. As we cross the Champs Elysées, my father reminds me how I used to call it the George Vée station.

We walk up the avenue to Rue Balzac, where a crowd has already gathered around the entrance to the cinema. They are the usual mix of actors, technicians, accountants, assistants, and others who took part in the shoot and the production. My father looks disconcerted; clearly he had a very different idea of what a "movie premiere" would be like.

"I can't believe I dressed up in your honor!" he grumbles, reproachfully eyeing the jeans, leather jackets, and T-shirts around him. He is dressed in a navy-blue blazer, a white shirt, and a pair of brown serge pants.

"Sorry, Dad, I know you were probably expecting a red carpet and TV cameras. This is just a few friends who had an adventure together, making a small film…."

"There are a lot of people for such a small film!"

"Some of them are friends of friends."

A tiny woman in her early thirties, who – with her boyish haircut, absence of make-up, and gray suit – is clearly the sort of girl my father would disapprove of, comes toward us.

"Philippe! Long time no see! How are you?"

She stands on tiptoe to kiss me on both cheeks and then turns to my father "Monsieur!"

"Caroline, my favorite sound engineer… my father."

"I thought so," she says, holding out her hand. "There's definitely a family resemblance."

While Caroline tells my father about the shoot in Morocco on which we met – and the famous story about the camels driven crazy by the explosions of grenades – I spot a young blonde woman behind her with a moonlike face, her eyes hidden behind enormous sunglasses. The sort of djellaba she wears does little to conceal the heaviness of her figure.

Catching my gaze, Caroline turns around.

"You don't know Charlie," she says, signaling to her friend that she should join us.

"Charlie, this is Philippe, a friend of mine, and his dad."

This last word, pronounced by someone who is a stranger to our family, has a peculiar effect on me. The little boy I used to be flashes into my memory, and I remember those afternoons when my dad – yes, my dad – would take me to see matinee showings of children's movies. Those outings were hugely important to me. How I savored the rare chance for a moment of intimacy with my father. I was desperate for such closeness. I knew, once the movie was over, he would become, once again, the man who intimidated and often terrified me, but I preferred not to think about that at the time.

"Are you okay?" asks the ever-perceptive Caroline. "You look sad or something."

"No, no, not at all. I was just thinking…"

"Uh-oh!" She bursts out laughing. "Your favorite joke, right? Come on, Charlie, let's get back to the others. Delighted to meet you, Monsieur."

"Dykes!" my father spits. "Look at that – they're even holding hands!"

"You have a problem with that?"

"Say what you want – that is not normal."

"What is normal, then?"

"They can do what they want in their own home, as long as they spare everyone else. There are children around. I'm telling you, it shouldn't be allowed."

"So, you think they should be punished for holding hands?"

"Probably just a fine, to start with. That'd make them think twice about it."

I am starting to feel discouraged. Was the vision I had of this week with my father nothing but a mirage? I love him – or want to love him, at least – and my mother's death has strengthened my determination to maintain this irreplaceable relationship, but my God, he makes it hard sometimes!

Thankfully, just at that moment, the usherette opens the doors. We are the first ones inside the movie theater and hesitating over which row we should choose, when I feel someone's hand on my shoulder. I discover Umberto behind me, in his usual leather sombrero, his brown face cloven by a broad smile. He, too, glances curiously at my father.

"My father, Umberto. The king of stunts."

"Ah! Pleased to meet you, Monsieur."

He sounds so polite. Funny, how the remnants of an education can still emerge from a mouth more used to spouting curses and obscenities in four different languages. It doesn't take him long to revert to type, however.

"You're one lucky bastard," he says in a low voice, "not getting mixed up in this shitty film. I'd rather fuck myself without lube than work for that director again. What a cunt. A real motherfucker. Anyway, ciao! I'm going to grab a seat close to the exit."

"He has a rich vocabulary, your friend," my father murmurs.

"Umberto's a good guy. We've worked together on a few movies."

Tapis Roulant is not a very good film, it has to be said. It is one of those comedies so unoriginal that you feel as if you have seen it a dozen times before. Most of the jokes fall flat, and the laughter comes from those who remember the mess-ups during shooting, the mispronounced dialog, the appearance of a boom in the picture, the actor's eyes straying toward the camera. The paying public is unlikely to be quite so enthusiastic about it, I think.

I lean close to my father and whisper "Sorry it's so bad, but it would be awkward to leave before the end."

Without a word, he nods and pats my knee with his hand. I needed that gesture. How many years have passed since he took me to see *The Return of the Pink Panther*?

"I've never been here before," my father says, and I am touched by the expression on his face. Demonstrative is not a word that usually comes to mind when I try to describe him.

We are sitting at a table in Fouquet's, each with a glass of champagne, compliments of the manager. The maître d' recognized me.

"Do you come here often?" my father asks as he glances at the menu.

"For work, yeah. Premieres, awards shows, that kind of thing. I don't have to pay."

"And a good thing too!" he smiles. "Have you seen the prices? Listen, are you sure you want to eat here?"

"It's my pleasure, Dad. You got all dressed up and I took you to see that piece of crap. So, what do you fancy? Do you still like oysters?"

"My God, it's been ages since I had oysters! But no, no, it wouldn't be reasonable."

Having overcome my discouragement earlier in the evening, I am happy to hear myself say "You remember what you said when you ordered a *kir* on our first night? It's not every day that you eat dinner with your son, or something like that. Well, for me, it's not every night that I go out with my father. So, Fines de Claires or Belons oysters? Or how about the seafood platter?"

I must admit I take great pleasure in the almost childlike look of amazement and delight on my father's face when the waiter brings us a platter of oysters, shrimp, whelks, and crabs, garnished with ice and seaweed. But the abruptness of his tone is like a punch in the gut.

"What are you smiling like that for? Are you mocking me because I'm not used to this kind of thing?"

"Don't be ridiculous."

I should be used to his aggressiveness by now, but the evening's charm is spoiled. The thoughts that have been pursuing me since the morning return to the forefront of my mind and I come to a decision. "You know," I say, "my friend Umberto, whom you met at the premiere... he started off in a circus. He was a knife-thrower. He used to give us demonstrations sometimes on set."

"Really!"

"That was how you got your scar, wasn't it? Throwing knives with a friend?"

Slowly, very slowly, his eyes fixed on me, he puts his empty oyster shell back on its bed of seaweed.

"Yeah. So?"

"How old were you?"

"Why do you ask?"

"Just curious. You told me, I'm sure, but I've forgotten. So?"

"I was thirteen. You do some dumb things at that age."

I force a smile and return to my shrimp, but I cannot silence the voice in my head: *I saw that photograph of you taken long after your fourteenth birthday, Dad, and you had no scar. Why are you lying to me? Why bother, about such a minor detail? It doesn't make sense.*

We finish our meal, but nothing is the same anymore. I feel as if I am a spectator to our conversation, rather than a participant.

On the way home, as we walk up the Champs Elysées before hailing a cab, my father suddenly asks, "Do you think I should find myself a girlfriend?"

"Why not? It's against nature to be alone. It's not a question of replacing Mom, I know that's impossible, but someone you could share the good and bad moments with... yeah, why not?"

"I'm not much of a catch. I've never been easy to live with and – let's be honest – I'm not likely to improve now."

"You don't have to live with someone. I just think... a girl-friend or just a friend... it would be good for you. Going out to a movie together, going on a trip."

"Actually, I've booked myself a cruise for the end of the year. I've paid the deposit already. It's made a dent in my budget, but I got a good price for the Roquette apartment, so..."

"You're kidding! Where are you going?"

"Athens and the Greek islands."

"Wow! For someone who talks about managing his days, you're really going for it!"

"You think it's a waste of my savings?"

"No! Not at all! I'm thrilled that you're going to enjoy your-self. Honestly! And you'll meet people on the ship...."

His face lightens with relief. So, my approval matters to him. At that moment, I have an idea.

Chapter Five

I gradually find a rhythm and the trash bags begin to fill more quickly. A cardboard box bearing the Orangina logo contains some old shoes; broken heels, holes in the soles, or just worn out. There are slippers and espadrilles, and two shoehorns. Destination: the dumpster. In another box marked "Philippe," I find some moth-eaten wool gloves, undershirts, shin guards, and my old soccer shirt. A shoebox contains some glasses cases, wallets and a purse, and some of my father's business cards for Meuble Moderne. Strange how they made such an effort to categorize and order a futile accumulation of stuff.

I recognize the games that we used to play on rainy afternoons during the holidays. My father rarely participated. I pause for a while when I find the white Monopoly box, the green Scrabble box, the cloth bag of dominoes, and I see my mother again, loudly denying that she had cheated after I had found her with her hand inside the Scrabble bag. I remember the day when, midway through a game, rather than going to the kitchen to fetch the glass of water she wanted, I stood behind the half-open door and watched as she blatantly changed her letters. I was outraged and demanded that she explain herself.

After first denying it, claiming that she was just rearranging her letters, she ended up confessing. Her justification was that she was testing me, to see whether I would be a good or a bad loser.

I don't know where I got my courage that day, but I remember refusing to believe her and accusing her of always cheating. Hadn't I recently caught her turning over the Trivial Pursuit cards as she set up the game?

She was put out at first, but then she took me in her arms and told me – I think I can remember her exact words – "You know, Philou, it's really not a big deal. It's just like a fairytale, where you create a world that is more beautiful than the real one. I'm just inventing a world where I win the game. I like fairytales. They help me to live."

Under a stack of *Paris Match* magazines tied up with electrical wire, the top cover showing a picture of Vanessa Paradis, I find a plastic box containing a boules set. A label stuck to the lid proclaims it the property of R. Feuillet, Impasse des Acacias. I gasp and sit down on a crate. Those heavy, silvered balls bring back the memory of a scene so brutal that it has lost none of its vividness over the years.

We had been invited by the Feuillet family to their little villa in Nice, where we had taken part in a friendly tournament with a few other neighbors. Roger Feuillet, a former colleague of my father's, his wife, and their pretty daughter, on whom I secretly had a crush, formed one team, while I was playing for the first time with my parents. There were three other teams taking part in this tournament, the prize for which was probably just a few glasses of pastis for the adults.

I relive the scene in all its details.

The Lamont team was playing against some neighbors who

were taking the game more seriously than we were. When my mother was caught blatantly moving the jack with the tip of her sandal, she simply denied it, swearing on her life that she had done nothing wrong. Our opponent, the local car mechanic, started insulting her. I remember the word slut, though I am sure I was ignorant of its meaning back then and must have found that out much later. My father demanded an apology, but the boorish mechanic just showered my mother with more curses. The epilogue was brief. My father took two steps toward him, his fists flew in a blur and the man crumpled to the ground, his face bloody, his jaw broken, before he could even lift his hands. I remember being proud of my father that day.

We never saw the Feuillets again. Why did my father keep his hosts' boules set?

Another glance around the cellar reveals a box that used to contain – and perhaps still does – one of the best birthday presents of my entire childhood: a Polaroid camera. Yes, here it is! It has not been used in a long time, of course, but I am going to take it home because for me it marked the beginning of a passion. Perhaps I even owe it my career? There is a padded envelope containing about twenty of my photographs. The colors have faded over the years, but the images remain as clear as ever. I look at them tenderly, noting that I was already concerned about composition. Here, my mother is bent over, brushing her shoes; here, my friend Francis holds a forbidden cigarette between his lips, protecting a match flame from the wind with his hand; here is a shot, taken from too far away, of my sexy neighbor rubbing sunscreen onto her breasts; and as for this one… I feel my throat tighten as I look at it. It shows my mother leaning on the windowsill. I took the picture from behind, intrigued by the possibilities of a backlit image. The light is warm but not dazzling; a summer evening, by the looks of it. Her hair flows down over her shoulders, haloed by the golden sunlight. The sheer curtains to her right are blowing slightly in the breeze. Surprised by the camera's click, my mother turned around and I saw – I will never forget this – her face bathed in tears. There are moments in life that nothing can erase. We stood there facing each other for several endless seconds before we hugged. My mother never told me what had caused her distress that day, simply reassuring me that I had done nothing wrong, that her tears had nothing to do with me. She made me swear not to say anything to my father. That photograph captures a painful moment, not only for her but for me. Not being able to understand, being helpless in the face of her pain… how terrible that made me feel!

I feel incapable of getting back to work. I decide I will go for a walk outside, perhaps drink a cognac at the bar around the corner. Alcohol in the morning? Yes. So?

I've made just a few steps down the corridor when my father stops me with his angry booming voice "Philippe! Your shoes, damn it!"

The two cognacs have weakened my determination to be obedient. Instead of complying, I keep walking and answer over my shoulder "There's no dog shit. It's only water, it's raining again."

"That's not the point. What is it you don't understand in no shoes in my apartment? Here you do what I tell you to do. Is that clear?"

I turn around. "First, you're leaving the apartment in a couple of days, Dad. It'll have to be cleaned anyway. Second, I'm not a kid anymore, so don't use that tone of voice with me. And third, please remember that I'm here because you asked me to help you with the move, OK? If you want me to go home, just let me know."

"Oh! So it's blackmail now!"

"Please don't use words you don't understand."

"You're nothing but an arrogant little shit, Philippe. Don't use your so-called education against me. I paid for it, remember?"

Now he's coming closer, raising his fist, as if ready to punch me in the mouth.

"Let's make this clear. As long as you're here, you do what I say, period!"

"Fuck you, Dad!"

The slamming of my bedroom door puts an end to this exchange. I lie down on my bed, keeping my boots on, something I would never do at home. God, why was I born to such an asshole? I hate this man, I really do. How could my mother have ever lived with this brute?

A glance at my watch. Lunch must be ready now, but there's no way I'll sit down to eat with this lout. I have work to do anyway, phone calls and e-mails. If I'm hungry in the afternoon, I can always go back to the café for a sandwich, and I definitely will not take my shoes off when I come back.

A nightmare wakes me in the middle of the night. My memories are confused and don't make much sense, as is so often the case, but what really jolted me out of my sleep after images of a pile-up on a highway was the vision of my father waving for help at a window of the highest floor of a flame-engulfed building. Firemen were climbing a huge ladder, but I was certain that they wouldn't reach my father in time.

My watch tells me it's 3:25, and I want to go back to sleep, but these final images won't let me rest. After long minutes of turning and turning, I finally get up and leave my room wearing only my Studio Plus tee-shirt and my shorts.

The apartment is quiet and dark, with only rays of moonlight coming from the kitchen window. My memory travels back to the years when, as a child, I used to walk to my parents' bedroom in the silent night instead of going back to bed after a visit to the bathroom. They always left their door ajar, a habit from the days when they kept an ear out for "Baby Philippe."

I was nine or ten years old then. I would push the door open and look at their shapes in bed. I don't know why I did that. I wasn't worried that they might have left and abandoned me—no, this routine just made me feel safe somehow. I would return to my room and go back to sleep.

In the kitchen I stop at the refrigerator for a glass of cold milk that I drink seated at the kitchen table, enjoying the silence. Funny how environment and circumstances dictate our actions—mine anyway. It's true, I never walk around in the middle of the night at home. Here where I spent my younger years, it seems natural, almost imperative.

Having left my glass in the sink, I leave the kitchen, ready to go back to bed, but I soon stop and turn around. Now I'm quietly headed for my parents' bedroom.

The door is ajar like it always was. I push it and noiselessly approach the bed where my father is snoring softly, his head turned toward me. During long minutes I stand there as my eyes slowly get accustomed to the darkness and my father's face becomes more distinct. It feels as if my mind is on hold, as no thoughts form themselves. I'm just standing there looking at his face free of the familiar angry frowns and creases.

Finally, I kiss the fingers of my right hand and move them towards my father's forehead, but I stop short of touching him. God knows what his reaction would be. He would probably bark at me. Instead, I blow a kiss on my fingers and quietly leave the room. The memory of my nightmare is erased now. I know I'll be able to sleep.

"Lunch will be ready in a moment!"

Sounds like an armistice. I too am ready to pretend nothing happened. I close a FaceTime session with Mireille, my assistant, and head for the kitchen where I'm greeted by a smell of garlic and onion. My father is busy at the stove.

"I'm making us a ratatouille for lunch," he tells me over his shoulder. "Go wash your hands and set the table."

The tone of his voice is redolent of my childhood and I can't resist a hint of mockery in my "Yes, Dad!" But he doesn't react, and I am glad about that.

A few minutes later, I am unable to conceal my astonishment "Wow, this is really good! I had no idea you could cook."

"Well, it was about time I learned."

"Yes, of course. Since Mom…"

"Oh no, it was before that. The first time she was hospitalized. You can survive on canned goods for a while, but five weeks… that's too much. It's nice to eat at Comme Chez Nous, but not every night."

"What? What are you talking about? Mom was in the hospital?"

"Yeah, the first time for a nervous breakdown. Well, it had some more complicated name, but anyway, she needed time to get over it. First in the hospital and then in a nursing home."

My fork is suspended in midair. For a moment I am speechless.

"But… how come I never knew about this?"

"You were shooting a film on the other side of the world."

"Okay, but there's such a thing as the telephone! And what about when I got home? You never even mentioned it!"

"Mom didn't want you to know."

"Why?"

He shrugs. "Apparently people who suffer from that kind of thing are always a bit ashamed of it. Even though it's not their fault."

"But I was… I'm her son!"

"Even more reason. She adored you, and she was afraid that you would think less of her. If she was still here, she'd be mad at me for having told you."

The ratatouille has suddenly lost its flavor.

"Wait a minute, Dad, you said the first time. You mean there were others?"

"One other time. But only for three days. The psychiatrist said it was just a precaution."

"And you still didn't say anything."

"That was her choice, as I said."

"Would you mind if I talked to that psychiatrist?"

"You'd be wasting your time. She wouldn't even tell me anything. Doctor-patient confidentiality. All she said was that your mom was fragile. Oh, really? Thanks for the information!"

I have no idea what to think. My brain must be like a snow globe after someone has shaken it to make the little white flakes fall. Fragments of memories flutter and twirl: images of my mother and, of course, the recollection of those tears as she stood by the window. It is not her sudden bouts of energy or enthusiasm – the reason for which often escaped me – that I find myself brooding over, because there was a certain charm in being swept away by such irrational joy, but the pain that I often used to see in her eyes. I would agonize over what I might have done or said to cause her so much hurt. I wanted to ask her forgiveness but did not know for what. It was not until I became an adult myself that I understood that her pain came from somewhere else, a mysterious place that I was never allowed to visit.

We sit there in silence for a moment before I gather my thoughts – and my courage.

"Can I ask you something?"

"Go ahead."

"Don't take this the wrong way, Dad, but is it possible that, deep down, she regretted sacrificing all the wealth and comfort of her childhood for…"

"For a guy like me, is that what you mean?"

"No, Dad. She always used to tell me that she made the right choice. What I mean is maybe she regretted it subconsciously."

To my surprise, my father grins.

"Don't worry. Conscious, unconscious, or subconscious, I can assure you that she never regretted anything."

I am about to ask him how he can possibly be so sure, but I decide to let it drop. It is not worth the risk of hurting him just to satisfy my curiosity.

"All right," I say, standing up to clear the table. "I have to make a few phone calls, and then I'll go back down to the cellar."

There was a time in my life when my father's revelations would have crushed me. I would not have forgiven myself for having been absent so often; I would have found a thousand reasons to punish myself and beg my mother to forgive me – for everything, for nothing, for anything. I would have been out for the count. Today, I am better able to distance myself from the irreparable damage of the past. I want to understand, obviously, but I am able to control my emotions. I owe this progress in part to Sophie, to our first separation.

We had been living together for two and a half years. Lucie, still a little girl at the time, was shuttling between us and her father, and we were trying to establish a solid foundation that would allow Sophie to gain custody of her daughter. We loved each other, there was no doubt about that, but the volatility of my character still worried her; she would bring the subject up occasionally.

That Sunday in April, Sophie had borrowed my car to visit her mother who, having just been widowed, lived alone near Fontainebleau. She came home in time for a microwave dinner. I had to catch a flight to Istanbul early the next morning, so I had already gone to bed.

When I left the house the next morning at 5:30, my car had

vanished. There was no point calling a cab, because I had left my plane ticket in the glove box to make sure I didn't forget it.

I went upstairs and woke Sophie who, at first still in shock, explained in a sleep-slurred voice that she had parked my car the previous evening on a crosswalk, intending to go back and find a better parking spot a few minutes later after putting her meal in the microwave. And then she'd forgotten all about it. Now the damn thing had almost certainly been towed, and I was going to miss my flight.

Mad with rage, ignoring her excuses, I took her by the shoulders and threw her out of bed, yelling insults at her as she curled up on the floor, her head in her hands.

My priority was to warn the producers, so I called her a stupid bitch, rushed out of the room, and slammed the door behind me.

One hour later, Sophie had packed her suitcases and disappeared from my life. "Your fits of anger have always seemed excessive," she wrote in her farewell note, "but I cannot live with a man who frightens me."

Perhaps I would never have been able to win her back, were it not for the incident that, five months later, almost endangered my career.

I was working on a movie in Poland with an English director named Mark Lessing; a tragic love story between Holocaust survivors. We had shot several scenes involving these lovers' children in the playground of a school and on a soccer field, with about thirty ten-year-old boys.

The shoot was entering its final week. I was supervising the lighting for a classroom scene where a teacher played by Max von Sydow was going to tell his students about the concentration camps. But the assistant director had seated the children at their desks too soon and they were becoming impatient. There was a risk of total bedlam. Off camera, the parents of these children were attempting to calm them down through words and gestures.

"Can you hurry it up?" the assistant asked me.

I coldly put him back in his place "If you think you can do a better job than me…"

We had just changed the positioning of the reflectors when a fight broke out in the first row. The parents intervened, but while one of them took his son's face in his hands and spoke to him, eyeball to eyeball, the other – a puny, bespectacled, ginger-haired man whom no one would have suspected of such violence – began smacking his son again and again. The poor kid protected himself as best he could with his hands and ended up curled in a ball underneath his desk.

Those two images – of Sophie, which still haunted me, and of this boy – became mixed up in my mind, though I was only barely aware of that as I strode angrily across the room. Grabbing the man by the back of his jacket, I attacked him just as he had attacked his own son. Soon, his face was covered in blood. God knows what would have happened had my colleagues not pulled me away and led me outside.

The day's shoot was postponed. That evening, Mathieu Straub, the producer who, long before this, had given me my first chance, came into my room at the hotel in Lodz.

"We've lost a day – you know how much that costs – and on top of that we're going to have to pay the guy compensation. But, believe it or not, I didn't come here to talk about money."

I learned a few hard truths that evening. "If you don't

face up to your problem," Mathieu told me, "your career is screwed. You're good at your job – as skilled as a cameraman as you are as a lighting director – and nobody would deny that. But you have to learn to control yourself. People talk in this profession, you know. Rumors spread fast. Producers have better things to do than manage your anger. So, do you want to talk about it?"

I lowered my guard and told him about the demon that sometimes takes hold of me. I talked about my father, about his temperament, which I feared I had inherited, about the environment in which I grew up, and in conclusion I told him about the incident that had led me to lose Sophie.

"I would do anything to get her back in my life," I said, "but I know that I have to change first, and that…"

Mathieu did not lecture me. Instead, he made me an offer. He would wipe the slate clean, allow me to finish this shoot, and even pay for any damages himself, if I agreed to see the therapist who had helped his brother-in-law in difficult circumstances. "You won't regret it," he assured me, holding me in his arms after I had given him my word.

It took me a year of work to learn to "hit the pause button," in the words of Frank Benamou, the therapist in question.

I recall our first meeting in a large, dimly lit room where an exotic scent lingered in the air. Benamou's appearance was disconcerting. He had white hair, but his face was like a doll's, without a single line. Dark eyes stared intensely from under thick eyebrows.

"What is your first memory of violence?" he asked me. "Go back as far as you can into the past."

As a child, I had been prone to fits of anger – I would kick out at my toys whenever I grew frustrated – but those memories, I suspected, were mostly of things my mother had told me. On the other hand, I do remember being expelled from the Henri Dunant middle school, the first in a series of expulsions. I was eleven years old and I was disciplined for having smashed my French teacher's chair over his desk and thrown the seat back through the window.

"What had he done to make you so angry?"

"He'd given me two hours in detention for copying from the boy next to me, which was completely untrue. I cannot bear injustice."

"What do you remember about your emotions that day?"

"The feeling that I was being swept up by a power that was greater than me. Like a dead leaf in a hurricane."

"And then?"

"Oh yes, the feeling that I was a thousand times stronger than I really was. Like Bruce Banner turning into the Incredible Hulk." I spoke in English "You wouldn't like me when I'm angry..."

The psychiatrist's lips twitched into a brief smile. "And then?"

I told him about the fight that had led to my expulsion from my second middle school and the beating I had been given in my bathroom.

Benamou taught me to envisage situations, and negative behavior, and to imagine positive alternatives, the kind that I would prefer to enact. Several times, he made me relive the moment of rage that had caused Sophie to leave me. I was transported back in time, furious at the idea of missing the preparation for the shoot in Turkey, and – not without difficulty – I managed to visualize myself listening to her explanations, accepting her excuses, admitting that anyone could make a similar mistake, wiping her tears of guilt from her face with my fingertips. Slowly, gradually, I learned how to tame my temper.

Benamou prescribed relaxation exercises; he taught me ways to control my breathing so I could compose myself in moments of anger, find within me the strength to take the necessary step backward. I hated those sessions, which a voice in the back of my head labeled a waste of time, but I had given my word to Mathieu and, most of all, I was desperate to win Sophie back.

For months, I had very little contact with Sophie. Our phone conversations to settle practical (and sometimes, I admit, imaginary) problems were generally discouraging. Her tone of voice was ice-cold.

One day I sent her a letter describing the efforts I was making and begging her to give me a chance by letting me take her out to dinner one night. She made me wait for her response, but in the end she agreed.

Sophie said she could see the difference in my eyes from the first moment she saw me again. "When I left you, you were an angry child," she told me. "When I found you again, you were an adult."

One week later, we were together again.

I find my father sitting in front of his computer, a very old Mac, checking the soccer scores. The time has come to deliver the surprise I've been thinking about since our dinner at the Fouquet's. I wanted this week to be special; this will be my special gift to my father, one we both will remember.

"Dad, I was just thinking about that cruise you booked. It's really a great idea."

Without looking up, he replies with a grunt of satisfaction.

"Actually, Dad, I was wondering if I might come with you on the cruise, if I can get the time off work. It'd be fun, the two of us together, don't you think?"

He suddenly loses all interest in the soccer scores. I watch my father's body stiffen as his eyes stare in confusion.

"But you couldn't take two weeks off work," he protests feebly. "Your career…"

"I checked my schedule. December shouldn't be busy. So, what do you think, Dad?"

I know my father and I didn't expect an explosion of joy, he's never been known for his spontaneity, but he looks like I've punched him in the gut.

"Wouldn't it be great?" I insist. "Father and son on a cruise to Greece!"

"Sure, of course," he says, still without looking at me. "But, you know, I still haven't made a decision. It's just a plan. A whim, you know. Maybe I'll just stay in my new apartment. If I feel good there, why not?"

"I thought you'd paid a deposit?"

"It's returnable any time until thirty days before the departure."

"Well, let me know as soon as possible, Dad, so that I block these two weeks on my calendar."

As I walk around the table, the taste of disappointment in my mouth, I notice the icon named Solange in the upper part of his computer screen.

"So, you and Mom shared the same computer?"

"Of course. We didn't need two."

"You didn't fight over it when you both wanted to use it?"

"Hardly ever. I used it during the day, when she was at work."

"And since… since it happened, you haven't looked through her files? Out of curiosity, you know?"

"I can't. I don't know her password." He turns to me and adds "And even if I did know it, I think it would be even more indiscreet, now she's not with us anymore."

"I see, Dad. Anyway, let me know about the cruise. Don't wait too long."

"Yes, I'll think about it."

Chapter Six

This morning, I find some still-warm pains au chocolat waiting for me in a basket covered with a paper napkin. Now that the elevator works again, my father says, there is nothing to stop him getting back into his old habits. As I sit down across from him, he adds "Did I ever thank you properly for the other night at Fouquet's?"

"Only twice, Dad."

"Oh, my memory! I can never even remember if I've brushed my teeth in the morning." He laughs sourly and adds "I doubt if I'll ever forget that seafood platter, though."

Encouraged by this exchange, I decide to say what's on my mind: "Dad, there's a subject we've been avoiding. That's natural enough, but there's something I'd like to ask you about."

His deep frown has intimidated me in the past, but today I am able to ignore it.

"I want you to tell me about Mom's last days."

He is silent for so long, eyes riveted to the surface of the coffee in his bowl, that I wonder if he is going to stand up and leave without a word, as he has so often done in the past.

"Why?" he finally asks.

"Going through all her belongings has really affected me. I need some way to come to peace with it all."

"What do you want to know?"

"I don't know... how she was the day – the weeks – before her suicide. Your last dinner together. What you talked about. Anything she was worried about. Anything you didn't notice at the time but remembered afterward. A sign, you know. Apparently, it's rare for someone to do that without leaving any kind of message or explanation."

"I don't know what to tell you. She seemed completely normal to me."

"And yet she must have planned it in advance, to take all those pills from the hospital. It wasn't a sudden impulse, I mean. You talked to her colleagues, didn't you? Surely they noticed something – a change in her behavior..."

He shakes his head. "No. Two of them came to offer me their condolences. They said they hadn't noticed anything."

"And the police?"

"You already asked me that. They found nothing suspicious. That's all they said."

"You must have some idea, Dad. Nobody does that and... not without a reason."

His shrug is intended to make me give up, but I don't.

"You know, I found a packet of letters at the bottom of her underwear drawer. I didn't read them, but they were postmarked 1978. She kept your letters."

"I didn't know that."

"There must have been at least thirty. Weren't you together back then?"

"In '78? It's strange, I have a clearer memory of what

happened years and years ago than of what I did yesterday…'78… oh, yes, of course. That was the year my boss sent
me to do a training course at the company headquarters." The
melancholy of his smile takes me by surprise when, in a suddenly lowered voice, he adds "We wrote to each other every
day, even Sundays. On Monday mornings we would mail two
letters."

"Tell me."

"There's nothing to tell. What do you expect me to say?"

"How things were between you back then. In my memories, you seemed close, but not the type of couple to write to
each other every day."

"We lived together. We didn't need to write to each other."

'That's not what I mean. I just never saw you as particularly… romantic."

"We were at the beginning."

"What happened?"

After a long silence when, eyes closed, he looks as though
he is lost in his memories, my father starts to speak. Strangely, I
have the impression that he is not talking to me, but to himself.

"It happens without you even noticing. A bit like gray hairs
or the lines on your face. You don't realize that a minor decision
can have such consequences. I remember, we used to go to the
movie theater together all the time in those early years, and we
would hold hands in the dark. I liked comedies, your Mom preferred romances – historical ones, ideally. So, she pretended to
like my movies and I did the same for hers. And then one day – I
can't even remember when or why – she said, 'Why don't you go
to see that movie without me? I have ironing to do.' I don't know
how I reacted. I imagine I must have been disappointed. All

the same, I remember enjoying the movie. Sure, I missed holding her hand, but it was good not to feel guilty about imposing my taste in movies on her. And then one day I told her that I'd rather watch a soccer game than see a movie about a princess in love. After that, it became a habit: we stopped going to the movies together, and we never held hands in the dark again. Hardly a tragedy, I know, but that's how you come apart as a couple, one thread at a time.' He gives a disappointed shrug. 'In fact, life is like that, when you think about it.

"What do you mean?"

"I mean, it passes… it slips through our fingers and we don't even realize, but there are moments when it gives you a shock. For example, you know I don't watch entertainment shows. I like documentaries, history programs. I always want to learn, and then… shit, where was I?"

"Life slipping through your fingers."

"Oh, yeah. See, I can't remember anything! But yes, if I happen to change the channel, I might see an actor, a comedian, or a journalist who I haven't seen for years. Every time, it comes as a shock and find myself wondering, what the hell happened to him? Or, why does she look like that? Because, in my head, that pretty girl, that handsome young guy, hasn't changed, and then suddenly there they are with gray hair or no hair, wearing thick glasses, jowly and fat, and I think, what a bitch life is! You can't win. Everyone loses. I hate games where the outcome is fixed in advance." Another grim laugh. "What am I babbling about?"

"You're not babbling, Dad. I like to hear you talk, even when what you're saying isn't cheerful. It doesn't happen that often, the two of us having a real conversation."

"Oh, and that's my fault, is it?"

It does not take much for his aggression to resurface.

"I'm not accusing you. That's life, as you always say. Doesn't alter the fact that I wish it were different."

He picks up the plates, bowls, and silverware, and sweeps the crumbs from the table with the side of his hand, his way of signaling that our conversation is over. As he stands up, he says "I'm not the same kind of person as you, Philippe. What happened cannot be fixed. If I could do something, anything, to bring Mom back, I would. But I can't, and you know it, so what's the point in talking about it? I'm not going to waste my final years racking my brains over questions that have no answers. Getting old is bad enough already; there's no need to make it worse."

"Oh, come on!"

"Come on, what? The way I live is to put one foot in front of the other, and not to turn around. Right now, I'm going to see my notary on the other side of town. You can keep emptying the cellar. And then this afternoon, I'd like to take a few boxes to the new place. Okay?"

I did not stay long in the cellar. My heart wasn't in it. My thoughts kept returning to that icon I'd seen on my parents' computer screen. I had not wanted to contradict my father the previous day, but he doesn't need to know my mother's password in order to access her personal files. I know how to go around it.

After filling just one trash bag, I persuade myself that going back upstairs does not necessarily mean I am going to do it. I am lying to myself, of course. Sitting in front of the old Mac, I move the cursor to the icon marked Solange without even consciously making a decision.

The dialog inside my head becomes deafening. One voice begs my mother to understand what I am about to do, explaining to her that I need to know. Another responds that I do not have the right to violate her secrecy.

I plead: *I had to come home, Mom, to realize how much I miss you! How can I get on with my life without seeking to understand? It's unbearable.*

She refutes me: *My decision to end my life was mine alone. It has nothing to do with you or your father.*

Before I cross the Rubicon, I decide to call Benamou. Over time, we have managed to build a more cordial relationship, even a sort of friendship. I was the one who moved things in that direction, although he did warn me: all intimacy is against the rules of his profession. Nevertheless, our interactions have become less formal.

"Is it really urgent?" Benamou asks. "I'm taking a train to Strasbourg tonight. I have two patients to see and I'm running late. I could see you next week."

"Please just give me five minutes on the phone."

"I have a feeling it'll end up more than that, but okay… go ahead."

Trying to put the conflicts within me into some sort of order, I end up telling him about all the events and memories of the last few days. "I feel lost," I say, in conclusion.

"I don't think you are lost, though. In fact, you're very lucid. You've noticed your father's contradictions, evasiveness, lies, but you are trying hard to preserve the perfection of this week because you have given it a sort of mythical value in your mind. Your desire for a memory that will survive your father is understandable, but it is possible to love him and remember him without turning him into a god or a saint. He is struggling through life, just like you and I."

"But I'm his son. Why lie to me? I feel sure he knows why my mother did it, and I need to understand."

"You asked him that and he denied it. What else can you do?"

Without mentioning my parents' computer, I simply wish Benamou a good trip and hang up. For all my temporizing, my decision was never really in doubt. Now, it is time. In a few seconds, I replace my mother's unknown password with another that I am not likely to forget: "Mom."

Ignoring for the moment the files lined up along the edge of the screen – most of which seem related to my mother's work – I open her e-mail inbox. I immediately note that it is has been full for a long time, because the latest messages are months old, most of them apparently spam. I don't waste time; what I need to read are the messages my mother wrote just before her death. I am desperate for clues.

The message at the top of the "sent" pile is, of course, the last one she wrote. It is addressed to <u>hip63500@yahoo.fr</u>. The text is brief: *Don't waste your time waiting. I will not wake up tomorrow, and nobody will be able to hurt me anymore.*

For several long seconds, I do not react at all. I am paralyzed. A thread of cold sweat runs from the back of my neck down my spine and all my muscles are clenched, aching.

This message is a reply to an e-mail signed with a single initial, M, and entitled "Small world," but in fact that title is the heading for the original message, the first in a long series. There are more than a dozen altogether. I have to read them in order, starting with the one at the bottom.

As I would prefer to study these emails in the privacy of my bedroom, I forward them to my own e-mail address. A good thing too, as the banging of the elevator door on the landing makes me jump. I close the laptop and head toward the entrance hall.

"My memory, my stupid damn memory," my father mutters, tossing his corduroy cap on the kitchen table. He got the wrong week, so it was a wasted trip.

"When I think that I used to know the phone numbers of all our suppliers by heart," he sighs. "And now…"

But anger is a more natural emotion for him than nostalgia, and it does not take long for his foul mood to explode.

"And what the hell are you doing up here?" he barks. "Why aren't you in the cellar?"

Lying to him is a natural reaction for me too. It became a reflex back in high school when I would come home an hour or two late.

"I came up to take a piss. I'm going back now."

"All right… to work, then. We'll eat lunch at one and we'll leave right after. So, get a move on!"

Yet again, the beltline is practically at a standstill.

"I'll ride my motorcycle next time I come to see you, Dad, because this road is a pain when you're in a car!"

"Oh, you're planning to come see me?"

"What do you mean?"

"I'm just wondering, because I can't say I've seen that much of you on Rue de la Roquette in recent years."

I could reply that, when I did come, he rarely looked happy to see me – he always had the expression of a man who is being disturbed at the worst possible moment – but why pick a fight? He, on the other hand, is like a dog that refuses to let go of its bone.

"Why would you suddenly want to visit me more than you did before?" he insists.

"The view, Dad. That magnificent view from your balcony of the rusting trains."

Apparently, I have scored a point, because he falls silent. He does not want to talk about what drew him to this place. Of course, I will go to see him. This week marks the beginning of a new chapter. The last one, probably.

In this silence, the questions that have been haunting me since this morning return to swarm inside my head. I am powerless to repel them. I know I have more to lose than to gain from this quest, because the truth is almost bound to be painful. But it is too late to turn back; the thought of deleting those emails from my computer is inconceivable. My whole being aches with the need to know.

"Well, would you look at that!" my father exclaims. "A Meuble Moderne van. So, they're still in business…"

"Why wouldn't they be? Did you think the whole company would collapse once you retired?"

"Of course not. It's just strange to see part of my past like that."

hip63500@yahoo.fr. Don't waste your time waiting. I will not wake up tomorrow, and nobody will be able to hurt me anymore.

"I'm sorry, Dad. What were you saying?"

"Just that I started life with a big handicap, because of my damn foster family! I should have got away from them sooner than I did."

"I thought you didn't like looking back."

"That's true. Still, everything would have been different if I'd had an education. Always having to bluff, to pretend you know where this or that country is or who wrote this or that book or who won this or that battle. I could fool other people, but never myself."

"Is that why you were so obsessed with *Historia* magazine?"

"Yeah, and it's also why I used to get so mad when you skipped school!"

Now my father starts fiddling with the radio, trying to find a station he likes; this is his way of marking a pause in the conversation. He is not used to revealing this much of himself. He scents danger.

hip63500@yahoo.fr. Who can be hiding behind that e-mail address? I could always send an e-mail, see who responds. If anyone does.

Inside the apartment, my father tries to turn the handle to the shutter on the living-room window.

"Let me do that," I say, watching him struggle.

"No! I have to be able do it on my own. Christ, these things are hard to work…"

Little by little, daylight enters the room as the badly lubricated mechanism screeches and creaks. I am about to call the maintenance department when I see my father shakily step backward and collapse onto a chair.

"Give me a minute," he says in a barely audible voice. "I'm just feeling tired."

With one hand under his elbow, I help him to stand up and lead him carefully toward the bedroom, where he lies down without protest.

I go to the bathroom and fetch a damp washcloth, which I fold in two and place on his forehead. Instead of pushing me away, as he would usually do, he offers a weak smile of gratitude.

"Shall I call the doctor?"

"No, please, don't make a scene. I'm just tired, that's all."

I pull up a chair and sit next to his bed. I put a hand on his arm.

"So, um, Dad…?"

He gives me a questioning look.

"I would like to have a key for this place. Well, a card. I don't want to feel like a visitor, if you know what I mean. Anyway… you never know."

His voice regains its strength now "One card is enough. All you have to do is tell me you're coming. I don't see the problem."

"But what if something happens? Like this…"

Our conversation seems to have brought him back to life. He suddenly sits up and puts his feet on the floor.

"I'm feeling better already," he says. "No need to make such a big deal of it."

"I'm not just talking about today. Another day, who knows what might happen."

"We're not there yet. One card is enough, I told you. Anyway, they have a copy downstairs."

Stubborn as a mule, my father.

"Well, since you're feeling better, I'm going to take a walk," I say, to escape my frustration. "I need to stretch my legs."

"Take your time."

The young black woman behind the reception desk is beautiful, with almond eyes and the kind of smile that beams from billboards.

"I'm the son of Monsieur Lamont, the new owner," I tell her. "Is it possible to have a second key – I mean a card – for his apartment?"

"Certainly, sir. I just need your father's signature."

She checks a screen as she speaks to me.

"In fact, there are already two cards, so this would be a third. Here is the form that your father will have to sign."

I sit on a bench next to an old lady. She is reading a large-print book and she smells of jasmine.

Benamou is right. Something inside me refuses to analyze the liberties my father is taking with the truth. I am not blind or deaf, but now is not the time to think it through or deduce anything, I decide. I can do that when I get back to my everyday life.

hip63500@yahoo.fr. Don't waste your time waiting. I will not wake up tomorrow, and nobody will be able to hurt me anymore.

Not only is my father over his "tiredness," but he has decided to taste the food at the Résidence Bellevue restaurant.

"I have to get used to the place sometime," he declares. "It may as well be now, with you."

There are about thirty tables covered with white tablecloths in the large dining room. The cream-colored walls are decorated with enlarged photographs of distant landscapes – palm trees, minarets, pyramids. The hostess to whom my father gives his room number is a woman in her early thirties. She is dark-skinned and wears a headscarf. Her name badge identifies her as Faizna.

"Give me a moment. I'll be with you right away," she says with a thin smile before moving away.

"Another one," my father remarks as he watches her.

"Dad, please!"

"So, they even have them here!" he says, ignoring my interjection. "I bet not everybody likes that."

"Not everybody thinks like you."

"Oh really? Wait for the elections."

I think about arguing but decide instead to grit my teeth and wait for the young woman to return and put an end to another episode that I would rather forget. Finally, she leads us over to a table at the back of the room.

"It smells of old people," my father says, after looking around at the other tables.

"I thought you'd lost your sense of smell."

"Inside, I can smell it," he says, tapping his forehead.

"These people might be your friends soon."

"So we can play dominoes together?"

"Actually, the average age is lower than I expected. Look at those two women to our right. Not bad at all. I bet they're still in their fifties."

"Late fifties."

"Younger than you, anyway. And those two over there: they look like they're having a good time."

I gesture with my chin at two jovial-looking men. The first is bald and his shiny head reflects the ceiling lights. He is very thin, with a large pair of glasses perched on his long nose. The other is red-faced, obese, and wears what is very obviously a toupee. Just as my father follows my gaze, the two men raise their glasses and clink them together.

"See?" I say. "Laurel and Hardy seem to be enjoying life."

At that moment, Hardy bursts out laughing so loud that people turn to stare.

"He's only laughing that loud so his friend can hear him," my father says. When I do not respond to this wisecrack, he asks me "What's up with you? Something bothering you?"

"No, I'm fine."

The truth is that I am struggling to stay in the moment. The hours that separate me from the moment when I will finally be able to read those e-mails feel interminable.

A sycophantic young man dressed in black comes to stand by our table, holding a colored pamphlet. He bows ceremoniously to my father.

"Allow me to introduce myself. I am Sylvain Rochemont and I am the leisure director at Résidence Bellevue. Welcome, Monsieur Lamont." Turning to me, he adds "Monsieur Lamont junior, I presume?"

If he is expecting my father to return his friendliness, he is soon disappointed.

"In this brochure, you will find a selection of entertainments to make your stay with us more agreeable. We are organizing a dance next Sunday evening. I hope to see you there. Bon appétit, and enjoy the rest of your evening."

"Dancing with old women? No thanks!" my father grumbles as the man walks away. "I don't know how to dance, anyway. It was never my kind of thing."

"But I thought you were a wonderful dancer!"

'What on earth makes you say that?'

"Mom told me."

"You must have been dreaming, Philippe. Have you ever seen us dance together?'

"No, but…"

"But what?"

"Oh, nothing. You're right – I must have imagined it."

But I did not imagine it, nor did I dream it. While pretending to read the menu, I explore my memory. I see myself again, sitting at my mother's feet, listening intently as she described her gilded youth. Not only did I never complain when she repeated the same stories, but I often asked for them: Mom, tell me again about the time your parents paid the circus people to put on a matinee show just for you for your birthday and the magician made your cake appear with all the candles on it. Yes, please, Mom, tell me again…

Or: tell me again, Mom, about how you met Dad.

After turning eighteen, my mother had finally been given permission to stay up until midnight for the Bastille Day dance in the suburb of Clermont-Ferrand where her family's mansion was located. Her father had initially insisted that her governess accompany her, but in the end, he had entrusted her to the care of the neighbors' eldest daughter.

So it was that my mother tasted freedom for the first time. I can still hear her describing the fireworks, the soldiers and firefighters in uniform, the musicians who would sometimes descend from their stage to parade across the dance floor. But most of all, she had spotted a wonderful dancer whom all the young girls were fighting over because they wanted to do the waltz or the tango with him. Their eyes had met and she had known before she even spoke to him that she had just fallen madly in love. Roland Lamont was not part of the local upper classes – far from it, in fact. He was an apprentice carpenter. He invited her to dance a slow waltz with him, and he was so assured that she forgot her own inexperience. More dances followed. The other girls could barely conceal their jealousy and hostility toward this unknown young woman who was monopolizing their idol. My mother was blown away by my father's passionate dancing style, his mastery of the most complicated steps, enabling her to follow them as if they were really quite simple. He walked her home and they arrived on the doorstep just as the twelfth bell of midnight tolled. She did not sleep that night, because she knew she now had to make the most important decision of her life.

"What are you daydreaming about, Philippe? The waiter just asked you if you've decided what to order."

"Oh, sorry. I'll have the pork chops."

"Philippe, are you sure you're all right?"

"Yes, why?"

"You look pale."

"Just feeling a bit tired."

The conclusion forms slowly in my mind. Perhaps it is an unimportant detail, but still… the fact is that either my mother lied to me then, or my father is lying to me now. But why on earth would my father feel the need to lie about being a talented dancer?

hip63500@yahoo.fr. Don't waste your time waiting. I will not wake up tomorrow, and nobody will be able to hurt me anymore.

Chapter Seven

I barely slept last night. Whenever I felt myself drifting into slumber, I would suddenly startle awake, covered in sweat, my laptop on my knees. In that half-conscious state, I at one point thought I had accidentally deleted the folder of my mother's e-mails. I hadn't, but it wouldn't really have mattered if I had, because every word of them is permanently engraved in my memory. I even remember all the spelling mistakes.

A ray of sunlight pierces the curtains and my head aches. Sitting on the edge of my bed, I feel incapable of getting up. It is past eight now, and my father is undoubtedly waiting for me in the kitchen to eat breakfast, but I cannot move. I am afraid of confronting reality and – I may as well admit it – afraid of sitting opposite my father.

As soon as we got back to the house yesterday, I rushed up to my room and opened my laptop. The first e-mail from hip63500@yahoo.fr was received by my mother nearly four months before the day she announced that she was going to kill herself. It came from a certain Marina and I had to read the messages that followed it before I could discern the threat that lay between its lines. I read and reread it:

Dear Lily… that was your name before, wasn't it? But don't worry, I'm not critisizing you, I changed my name too. I went back to my old name, but unlike you I didn't leave Issoire. Anyway, it's a small world, isn't it? Especially now, with the internet. I found you by chance on Facebook the other day. Incredible, eh? I was looking through a friend's photos, and in one of them she was sitting in a nice restaurant. There were six people around the table. At first I didn't really pay much attention, but then I went back to that photo. Of course, you've changed and your hair is gray now, but it was your eyes and your smile that I reconized I can't explain how. And then I saw your scar and I remembered what happened and I knew that I'd found Lily again. My friend told me that you call yourself Solange now and that the man to your right is Raoul. So you married him, eh? Congratulasions. And I learned lots of other things too. You've done well for yourself, I hear. Reply soon – we have a lot to talk about.

Lily. Lily. How many times did I reread that name? My head was spinning. I felt as if I were on a cliff edge, terrified of leaning toward the chasm below. Those two syllables echoed inside my head.

My mother had tried to ignore this message, but several others had followed and their tone had become more urgent. The one that forced her to reply was effectively an ultimatum:

So Lily, obviously I haven't made myself clear. How would you feel if I told everyone about our years at the Bar du Chat Noir? I have a lot less to lose than you do. You and

Raoul got out in time, and in fact it was what happened with you two that messed everything up – the bar had to close after that. All the same, I doubt weather you'd really want me to share my memories of your time there. My friend told me all about you. I know where you live. I know you have a good life. I also know you have a son. I wonder if he knows about your past? So, Lily, time to get in touch with me before I do something you'll regret.

Our years at the Bar du Chat Noir!

Once, years before, I had felt the terror of wandering into an unknown place, populated by ghosts. I must have been about ten when my parents took me to that amusement park in the Bois de Vincennes. When I refused Dad's offer to enter the Haunted House, I remember, he called me a coward and forced me to ride it with him, ignoring my mother's protests. The skeletons and ghosts shrieking and moaning as they appeared suddenly out of the darkness, the spiderwebs touching my face, the rumble of thunder... I was so frightened, I ended up vomiting. But even that ride was nothing compared to the dark tunnel through which I was moving now.

My mother's first e-mail read:

Hello Marina. Of course, I remember you and I hope that you made a good life for yourself, that you are happy and healthy. As you can guess, I did everything I could to forget those years. Why would you want to stir up the past? Are you expecting something from me? Solange.

The reply came the next day.

Lily, thank you for finally replying. Please don't call your-self Solange with me. What am I expecting from you? To share some of today's good things by remembering yester-day's bad things. My state pension is hardly enough to live on. Make me an offer and I'll see if it's enough.

To which my mother had responded:

You're fooling yourself if you think I'm rich. I work in a hospital and Raoul is retired and we don't have much money left over after paying for the essentials. I could prob-ably scrape together three or four thousand euros if that would help, but I'd have to find a way to get the money to you bit by bit without Raoul noticing. I don't know how I can manage that. I hope you'll understand.

Marina did not understand.

I would almost have prefered it if you'd told me to piss off rather than offering me 4,000 euros. What do you take me for? I'm not asking you for charity, I'm asking you to share what you have. Be serious.

Reading this, I wondered if my mom had ever thought, even for just a minute, of asking for my help. She wouldn't have had to answer my questions. If she'd told me it was im-portant, but that she couldn't tell me any more than that, I would probably have imagined the worst – an operation, can-cer, God knows what – but I would have done my best to help her. But no, she preferred to negotiate, making a series of offers for quarterly payments, all considered too low by this Marina woman. Did my father finally get wind of this? There is nothing in what my mother wrote to make me believe so. And I couldn't possibly ask him. There is no way I could admit that I had stolen information from his computer.

Fifty thousand euros was, ultimately, the sum demanded by Marina. As a show of goodwill, she said she would accept the money in two payments – one before the end of the month, the other at the end of December. This demand was enough to convince my mother that her nightmare was not going to end. Three days later, she sent Marina her final e-mail. The day after that, she committed suicide.

⸺∞⸺

My father's fist makes the door shake.

"Philippe, you're not still in bed, are you? You'd better get up if we want to finish up today!"

I mutter an apology, then stagger to the bathroom, where I splash my face and neck with cold water.

Putting on a pair of jeans and a T-shirt, I wonder: Why does the idea of confronting my father fill me with such anxiety? Have I really not managed to put my childhood behind me? The truth will have to come out, that's the reality, and I can't ignore it any longer.

A few minutes later, I join my father at the kitchen table. He glances at his watch and grumbles "So?"

"Sorry. I didn't sleep last night."

"Problems?"

What if I replied *Nothing important, Dad, I just found out that Mom's name was Lily and she was being blackmailed by someone called Marina because she used to work at the Bar du Chat Noir. Oh, and this Marina remembered you too.*

"No, not at all. It just happens to me sometimes."

He pushes the basket toward me. Inside are two pains au chocolat.

"Are you sure you'll be done downstairs by tonight?"

"I'm almost finished. I should even have time to go to a meeting this afternoon. So, I might be a bit late for dinner."

"And tomorrow?"

"I'll leave early."

"Tell me what time. I'll set my alarm." He pauses, then adds "This will be our last breakfast together."

There is a catch in his voice that suggests he is feeling an emotion I had not thought him capable of. For years, I have lived with the image of my father formed during my childhood and adolescence, an image whose details have been erased by time. Only the main features remain in my mind, probably those engraved deeply in my memory by powerful emotions. The picture of him in my mind is not a caricature, more a rough sketch. But I now know that this picture is based on lies.

Who were my parents really? I am starting to think of myself as an insect trapped inside a jar; I keep bumping into invisible walls. And to think that my father, observing me from above the rim of his bowl, knows all the answers – and I can't interrogate him! But then what is to say that he would answer me truthfully anyway?

"You really don't look well, Philippe."

"Don't worry, Dad. Once I get started, I'll be fine. I often don't get much sleep when I'm on a shoot, you know. I've learned to kickstart myself in the mornings."

"And tonight, for our last dinner, we'll go back to Vittorio, where we had our first dinner this week."

"It won't be our last dinner."

He nods to express his satisfaction at this response, then opens his newspaper.

"The obituaries?"

He laughs silently. "I look at the weddings too. To see if the *folles* below are going to dare…"

I don't even bother protesting.

"Why are you smiling, Philippe?"

"Nothing. I was in the elevator with them the day before yesterday. They asked me how you are."

"Why the hell should they care? My life is none of their damn business."

And what about me, Dad? Is your life any of my damn business?

Gusts of rain spatter against the windows of the café where Josiane Faillard has agreed to meet me. A colleague of my mother's at the Saint Antoine hospital, her e-mails have led me to believe that their relationship was more than merely professional. It was Josiane who suggested the Blouses Blanches café, a short walk from the hospital's main entrance. "My headquarters," she called it.

I know this place well because I often came here to meet my mother during the cold war with my father. Midway between a brasserie and a pizzeria, it is a place I like because of the wildly colored décor. Through the condensation on the window and the whipping rain, I can make out a constant flux of men and women emerging from the hospital under umbrellas. Some head toward the metro station while others choose between Les Blouses Blanches and its main competitor, Mon Café.

"Philippe Lamont?"

I look up and see a short woman with a severe face, her white hair covered by a transparent plastic hat. In my haste to stand up, I knock my chair over.

"I beg your pardon, Madame. You told me in your e-mail what you looked like, but I didn't see you come in."

Her smile corrects my first impression. "We all look the same in these things," she says, removing a sort of poncho, also plastic, which she drapes over the back of her chair.

"How did you recognize me?"

"Solange used to keep a photograph of you on her desk. Not a recent one, but you haven't changed that much. I saw you at the funeral too."

"You were there?"

"Of course. But I was too upset to introduce myself. And, well, I'm not really at ease in social situations."

I raise an eyebrow at this, and she smiles. "It's true. I have a good rapport with my patients, but once I get out of the hospital…"

I smile back at her. We order two teas and I ask, "Madame, if I understand correctly, you…"

"Your Mom called me Josiane. Her son should do the same."

"Thank you, Josiane. You work in the same department where my mother worked, is that right?"

"Internal medicine, yes."

"And you were friends?"

She nods sadly. "Yes. It gave me a terrible shock."

For a moment, I don't know where to lead our conversation and we sit in silence. It is Josiane who rescues me. "What do you want to know?"

"I want to understand."

"Of course. We asked ourselves so many questions too."

"Who is 'we'?"

"There's a small group of us, you know, very close. Doctors, nurses, secretaries, we spend our lives together. But for me, in particular, it's because my…"

She lowers her head and sighs. I can tell she is finding it hard to continue this conversation. I respect a moment of silence, and then probe her "Because your…?"

"Because my granddaughter disappeared the day after her seventeenth birthday. She'd been living with me since my daughter's divorce and that day she ran away, leaving a note saying she was sorry. That was all. No news for four months. God, it was horrible! I wouldn't wish that on anyone."

She smiles bravely. "I'm not exactly a big woman, but I somehow managed to lose sixteen kilos. There was hardly anything left of me."

"I'm sorry, that sounds terrible. So, after four months?"

She looks up and forces another smile.

"And three days! She came home. She didn't want to say anything except that she'd been with an older man. The reason I'm telling you this is because your mom was different from everyone else, friends and family. She was the only one who really seemed to share my anguish. The only one where it wasn't just words of comfort."

"That was one of her qualities," I say, fiddling with a spoon.

"Yes, she was deeply sensitive, but wait – there's more. One evening—I will never forget this—Aline had just come back and I asked Solange to come eat dinner with us, because I wanted to ease the tension a little. Suddenly, without any provocation, Aline shouted that nobody could understand. She left the table, saying we had no idea what she'd been through. And your mom just burst into tears. I didn't know what to do. I ended up having to console her."

"Did she explain?"

"No, but when I questioned her, she whispered that she didn't need to imagine."

'What did she mean?'

"I don't know. She just kept repeating 'I don't need to imagine' before rushing home, as if she couldn't bear to answer any more questions. And afterward I never dared mention what had happened that night. I had the feeling it was a very raw nerve and I should be careful not to touch it. I didn't want to…"

Josiane breaks off, and I follow her gaze to my right hand. My fist is clenched and my fingers have twisted the spoon out of shape. I force a smile, as if this were just a harmless pastime. The truth is that, while Josiane was speaking, my mother appeared, every bit as real as if she had been sitting in front of me. I recognized the distress in her eyes. The lines around her eyes deepened and her chin trembled. "I don't need to imagine," she whispered. I heard her voice, and for an instant her pain brought her back to life for me.

Josiane shrugs and shakes her head, in recognition of the painfulness of life, then says "So, your questions…"

"Did you notice any change in her toward the end?"

"Well, you knew your mom. It was in her nature to have highs and lows, but she was well cared-for and her treatment kept her pretty stable. All the same, it's true that her mood grew darker over those last two or three months. We were close enough that I would question her, but she just withdrew into her shell. I tried to divert her – you know, going to the movies together, inviting her to lunch – but nothing helped. I'm not saying that I expected what she did, of course I didn't, but while the news came as a shock, it wasn't a complete surprise."

"I see. And you went to see my father, I believe?"

"Of course. With another colleague, Lorraine."

"How did he seem?"

"Stoical. There's no other word. Determined to hold up. A solid man who hides his emotions."

"Did she ever tell you about him?"

Josiane Faillard frowns at me. "What do you mean?"

"I don't know… it's fairly normal, isn't it, to talk to a friend about your life beyond work?"

She shakes her head, pensive. "It's strange that you should ask me that, because I remember remarking to her that she never mentioned her husband. She replied that there was nothing to say after so many years, and the two of them didn't talk much anyway. She said her husband didn't like chatter. I remember trying to imagine your parents eating their meals in silence. When my husband was alive, we would always tell each other about our days, but apparently your parents were different, if you know what I mean."

I know all too well.

Josiane glances at her watch. She sees me notice this and explains "Aline is better now and she's doing well at college, but

I always feel like I need to be at home for her by seven-thirty. I know it's silly, especially as she's probably out with her friends, but I never really got over what happened before."

"I understand. Two more questions, that's all."

"Okay."

"Did she ever mention Issoire?"

She looks at me blankly.

"It's a town, in Auvergne."

"Oh… no, never."

"And now the trickiest one. Do you have any idea how she could have got hold of all that Rohypnol?"

She shrugs. "I can only guess, but stealing a few prescription drugs is not too difficult for a nurse."

"I checked, though, that particular medicine is not available anymore."

"It was then."

As Josiane Faillard wraps up in her poncho, I stand up and kiss her on both cheeks. "From my mother," I say.

Nibbling a breadstick, I watch my father converse with Vittorio. The two of them keep glancing over at me. What could they be talking about?

I have set another trap for my father, but this time I feel no shame. We were sharing the first glass of a richly scented Amarone when I heard myself say, in a voice as neutral as if I were talking about our next family vacation "I've got those three ads to shoot in Brittany, and then they're sending me to take photographs for another project. A week on my own, walking in Auvergne."

"Oh, really? Whereabouts?"

"Issoire and the area around it."

We were sitting side by side on the fake leather bench, but I could see my father's face in the mirror facing us. I noticed his expression freeze and pretended not to pay any attention to his sudden silence. I waited for a moment, and then "But I was thinking, Dad… that's where you're from, isn't it?"

"No, I was born in Murol."

"But it's in the same region, isn't it?"

"I suppose."

"And Mom grew up in a wealthy family in Clermont-Ferrand – is that right?"

"Yes, that's right."

"Where have I got this idea that you used to talk about Issoire when I was a kid? It came back to me when they offered me this job."

Instead of replying, my father abruptly got to his feet, muttering that he had to go to the toilet. On the way back, he started chatting with Vittorio, who – being a good Italian – accompanies his words with incessant hand movements.

And to think I was expecting this week to bring me closer to my father! Our lives are inescapably connected and his death will leave me an orphan, but I am no longer sure I even know him. He has learned to tame his temper, but the brutality of his nature remains. As for his lies and silences, what dark mystery can they be hiding? I am, I think, like those archeologists who once suspected that Nefertiti's tomb was hidden behind Tutankhamun's.

One of the waiters signals to Vittorio for help and he walks over toward him while my father returns to his seat.

"Vittorio is going to move," he says, sitting down next to me. "His rent keeps going up. He showed me the letter from his landlord – a Monsieur Schwartz, would you believe? Yet another one who's not from around here!"

"Dad!"

"All right, never mind that. Anyway, we were reminiscing. About the night when we celebrated your birthday and they got the number of candles wrong. Your mom got upset – she said she was already sad about you growing up, there was no need to add to the number of your years! You remember that?"

"Vaguely. Tell me, Dad, do you often think about Mom?"

"What do you think?"

"Were you happy together?"

He turns to frown at me. "You ask some strange questions."

He grabs the menu and moves his glasses from his forehead to the end of his nose while I brood over the fact that he did not answer my question. I realize in that moment that I have made a decision. I have no choice now. I owe it myself and to the memory of my mother to find out the truth.

I must go to Issoire.

Chapter Eight

I don't know what it feels like or how difficult it is to be a father. What I'm living with is the challenge of being a stepfather.

In spite of my sincere affection for Lucie, I'm always walking a fine line. If I were her father, there would be conflicts, I know that, but our relationship would be dictated by clearly understood rules. Instead, what I really am is the man in her mother's life and she likes to remind me—sometimes with just a look—how limited my authority over her is.

I do not wish to paint a negative portrait of Lucie. Definitely not. She is smart, sensitive, funny, and has a good heart, but her personality is strong and she's in the process of becoming a young woman which, I'm told, is not an easy journey.

"There's a very lucky guy somewhere who won't know how fortunate he is until he meets you," I told her last week and I felt Sophie's hand squeeze my knee under the table.

Tonight, we just finished the appetizer, a salad of tomatoes, basil, and mozzarella, and Lucie has already picked up her cell phone several times.

"You know, Lucie," I say as calmly as I can, "dinner is the

only time when we're together as a family. Your phone is not a guest, it's not invited. Would you please put it back in your bag?"

"I'm not making calls."

"I know that, but you keep checking your screen as if we're not here. And you were also typing something."

"My dad has no problems with the phone. He does the same all the time."

"Your father does what he thinks is okay. That's not for me to judge. When you're here, though, you're with us. It's our home, it's about the three of us."

"Philippe is right, you know, honey," Sophie says while reaching for her daughter's hand, but Lucie pushes her chair back, rises, and stalks off to her room. Before slamming her door, she turns around. "Enjoy your meal."

With a sigh, Sophie goes to the kitchen and comes back a while later with a cheese omelet and white asparagus. "We'll save some for her," she says. Then she asks, "Were you able to reschedule your trip?"

"I'm afraid not. There are other people involved. Locations scouting, you know."

"You won't be here for your birthday."

"I know. That's the curse of this job. When have I ever been in Paris for my birthday?'

"Yes, I know, but Lucie has a surprise this time."

"I think I'm on her shit list right now."

"Don't be silly, she loves you. That was just her being sixteen."

"A surprise, you said. What is it?"

"Try looking up surprise in the dictionary!"

"Touché!"

"You really couldn't find another time?"

"A week or so won't make a difference. We can still blow out the candles."

I'm uncomfortable because I didn't tell the truth. I still find it impossible to share my doubts about my mother's suicide and my father's inconsistent answers. They are at the very heart of my identity. Sophie is not only my life partner, she's also my best friend, but putting my fears into words is still too hard. One day, soon I hope, I'll tell her everything, but I'm not ready.

I had to wait for a window of opportunity in my schedule. When I saw that I could take a couple of days off from the Charlize project, I didn't hesitate. I informed the production team, contacted an assistant I knew in Auvergne, booked a hotel, and bought a train ticket.

"Good morning again, sweetheart," I say when I come out of the bedroom, pulling my carry-on behind me.

I love Sophie's look in the morning when she wears her sky-blue robe and hasn't put on her make-up. "When I think of the work we girls put in every day to be glamorous and sexy for you guys," she remarks when I tell her how much I love her au naturel.

There are four plates, four glasses and four cups on the breakfast table. "Why four?" I ask.

"I forgot to tell you. Minh is here to prepare for their exam. They're in Lucie's room."

Just as Sophie is pouring the freshly-squeezed orange juice, Lucie comes out with Minh, a lovely Vietnamese fifteen-year-old who is her best friend. Minh is petite, her skin is luminous. Her round face is framed by wonderfully silky jet-black hair.

Both girls come to me for morning kisses before sitting down at the table and immediately resuming their conversation, a collection of gossip about their schoolmates, to which I pay no attention, lost as I am in what might be awaiting me in Issoire.

"Honey! Are you daydreaming again? Minh just asked you a question."

"Sorry, Minh. I was lost in my thoughts. So, your question?"

"Yes, Lucie was telling me you're off to Auvergne. I was wondering if it's a nice place to visit."

"I don't really know it very well, Minh. My assistant will be there to show me around."

Now Lucie has left the table and runs back from her room with a package wrapped with a pink ribbon. "Here, Dad. This is for your birthday."

Sophie and I lock eyes. I struggle to act cool, but I'm shaking inside. This is the first time Lucie has ever called me Dad.

"I know we'll celebrate when you come back," adds Lucie, "but you should have it now to read on the train."

I hug and kiss Lucie. "It's not much," she says. "It's just that we studied *L'étranger,* by Camus, in class, and I thought it was really great. I hope you haven't read it."

"No, Lucie, it's a famous novel, but I never had the chance. Now I do and I'm looking forward to it. It's a lovely idea."

The looks that Sophie and I exchange tell everything that needs to be told.

———∞———

My excitement is like that of a bloodhound on the morning of the hunt, as the TGV carries me far from Paris and the landscape speeds past in a blur of rain, but it is mixed with a sort of dread about what exactly I might discover when the hunt is over.

I did try to convince myself that this quest was just a waste of time and energy, a game that I could only lose; nothing could change the past I should just forget the whole thing. But, in the end, I could not extinguish the blaze that was consuming my mind.

I have imagined so many different scenarios. What if my mother, in love with my father, had found a way to escape her parents' surveillance and had gone to meet him in his favorite bar? There, they could have met Marina, an employee, perhaps a waitress. Something bad could have happened one day – an accident, a fire, a hold-up. They could have witnessed it and... but no, none of this would have been enough to inspire blackmail half a century later.

Or what about if my father was working as a barman to make ends meet and my mother went to meet him at the Chat Noir... but there too, I am left with the same absurd supposition.

What if? What if? I shuffle and reshuffle the cards, swapping roles, inventing encounters. My brain will give me no rest.

I pat my jacket, hoping to find some mints, and come across the book that Lucie gave me as an early birthday present.

I open *L'Etranger* to the first page.

"Mother died today." The opening line affects me like a cold shower. I do not read any further. As I close the book, my cell phone vibrates inside my pocket. On the screen, I read my father's name. We have quickly returned to our usual mode of communication: a series of exchanges on practical information and general observations. The moving company people unhappy with the tip he gave them; the leaking toilet; his farewell to the *folles* on the third floor who, spotting him close to the van, wished him good luck – "but it sounded like 'good riddance' to me!"; the monthly fire drill in his new building; climate change and the end of the world as we know it.

"You're such a pessimist," I told him last week.

He sniggered. "As you get older, you notice that the difference between pessimism and realism is wafer-thin."

I am about to take his call, but I change my mind. The thought of talking to him while I am on my way to Issoire is too much. Part of me feels as if I am betraying him. Who knows what I will discover in that town?

The rain has stopped and I let my thoughts wander as I stare out at cows in fields, the rooftops and belltowers of distant villages. Then I put in my earbuds and choose Clara Haskil's famous rendition of Schumann's piano concerto. I like jazz, rock, and even rap in homeopathic doses, but nothing soothes me like classical music. That concerto was my mother's favorite.

The train comes to a halt in Clermont-Ferrand station and I suddenly wake from a deep sleep. I did not even hear the announcement. Around me, everyone is standing, gathering their bags. A pretty young woman, who must have sat opposite me while I was asleep, smiles at my disconcerted expression. "Sweet dreams?" she asks.

A ticket inspector bangs on the window. I read his lips: Get off the train.

I am one of the last to leave. Ahead of me, the crowd of travelers presses toward the exit. A man stands at the end of the train, looking lost, holding up a sign that reads Philippe L. This stranger is older than the assistants I usually work with; he must be in his sixties. He cannot be the same man I talked to on the phone. A stocky man with a rugged face, he is wearing an open waistcoat over a white shirt with the sleeves rolled up. I could imagine him as a shepherd, leaning on a staff, surveying his flock in the mountains.

I go over to him. "Sorry, I nodded off. So, Tony couldn't make it?"

"No. I'm his father, Antoine, and I'll be replacing him, if that's all right with you. He had an offer for a series of TV ads. He told me that your work here is not related to the cinema, so I volunteered to take his place."

I must look uncertain, because he adds "Actually, if you're looking for information on Issoire in the '70s, I'll be more useful to you than my son."

I shake his hand. "Sounds good, Antoine. Let's go!"

The humidity is oppressive, and I take off my jacket while we walk through the parking lot. "Is it normally like this here early June?"

"Not at all," says Antoine, slapping himself on the back of the neck. "We've never seen anything like it. The worst thing is the mosquitoes."

He has not rented a car, as I suggested to Tony. "I've got my son's Golf," he explains. "I dropped him off in Chamalières this morning. You don't need me for long, right?"

"Forty-eight hours max."

Antoine uses the thirty-minute journey to persuade me

that he is the perfect man for the job. He used to deliver consignments of the *La Montagne* newspaper to Issoire and its surrounding area, and he made a few friends at the paper, a couple of whom still work there.

"I have access to their archives," he assures me. "Not only that, but because I do them favors like going to the town hall to get information, I know the people there too. How does that sound?"

He holds out his hand, I shake it.

"Oh, I almost forgot!" he says. "Tony gave me this note for you. He had time to go to the town hall after talking to you."

He hands me a sheet of graph paper. Three lines have been scrawled on it in capital letters.

"Nobody can read his handwriting," Antoine remarks. 'That's why he prints it like that. Even at school he…"

But I am not listening anymore. Time has lost its shape. For a few seconds that seem to stretch out like hours, my brain refuses to decipher the letters that stand there clearly before my eyes. At last, it has to surrender, abandon its resistance, and the words are able to deliver their message. As I stare at those lines traced in ballpoint pen, I am paralyzed, incapable of forming a single thought.

A moment later, the shock is over and I am able to analyze the words on the page, to understand their meaning. Putting my hand to my mouth as if to stifle a groan or a cry, I numbly tell Antoine to stop as soon as possible.

"Something wrong?" he asks.

I shake my head and point at a Total gas station in the distance. "Stop there!"

As soon as the car comes to a halt in the parking lot, I

struggle to free myself from my seatbelt and then get out of the car without answering Antoine's barely heard questions. My lungs need air; my whole body is desperate to escape the suffocating sensation that grips me. I stride away, wind-milling my arms, taking deep breaths as I try to overcome the horror that those lines have provoked in me. I see them again, those coarsely written letters: BAR DU CHAT NOIR, A BACKSTREET BROTHEL, WAS CLOSED ON NOVEMBER 5 1974 AFTER A POLICE RAID. THE POLICE WERE CALLED BECAUSE A CLIENT WAS STABBED TO DEATH OUTSIDE THE ESTABLISHMENT.

A whorehouse! A murder! Some kind of self-defense mechanism in my brain forces me to postpone thinking about this. For now, I am frantically trying to build a dam to stem the flood of emotions that threatens to drown me. I realize it is too late for this, but I have to find some semblance of calm. A brothel! *Don't think,* I tell myself; *don't imagine it; don't draw any hasty conclusions; there must be an explanation.* Thinking is completely impossible for now. The Chat Noir was a whorehouse! I lock this information in a strongbox at the back of my brain and decide I will not open it again until I have regained my sang-froid.

"Feeling better?" Antoine asks when I get back in the car.

"Just a bit carsick. I'm fine now."

He shoots me a long look, inviting confession, but what could I possibly tell him?

"All right," he says, resigned. "I'll drop you at your hotel and go back to Clermont. I'll see if anyone still knows me at *La Montagne* and if they've got anything in their archives about this. We can meet for dinner, if you like. The hotel restaurant is supposed to be good."

I do not have the energy to reply to him, so I just nod instead.

Le Relais is a modern and welcoming hotel, facing a lush park on the other side of the street. My room is comfortable, but there is no way I can bear to remain a prisoner of its four walls. Too many emotions, too many questions are whirling through my mind. I am desperately seeking a simple, plausible explanation that could put an end to this nightmare.

Walking along the banks of the Couze river helps me to find, if not peace, then at least a semblance of composure. I have always loved the atmosphere of these small French towns. Often I have told Sophie that I could see myself, one day, settling in Bourgogne or by the Loire, for example. She does not take these romantic dreams seriously. "You'd die of boredom," she always says.

My cell phone vibrates. Antoine! Does he have any news?

"No," he says. "I put out some feelers, though. We'll know more tomorrow. I told them it was urgent."

He is on his way back to town, earlier than expected, and he suggests we meet at his favorite bistro on Place de la République. "It's right in the center of town," he tells me. "You can't miss it. Plus, it'll help you get your bearings."

So it is that we meet on the terrace of a wine bar where Antoine is obviously a regular.

"A glass of your favorite rosé," the owner suggests. "Nice and cold in this hot weather."

My cell phone vibrates. My father again. I couldn't possibly speak to him now.

"So, what happened back there? Are you feeling better now?"

"Yeah, just carsick, like I said. And I'm pretty tired."

I catch him looking at my hands and hastily stuff them in my pockets.

Antoine takes his time, but, like a bad actor, he overdoes it. He eyes a ray of the setting sunlight filtered pink through his wine, then casually examines his fingernails and utters a sigh of contentment. Finally, unable to bear it any longer, he gives in to his curiosity.

"Maybe it was what you read on Tony's note that took you by surprise," he suggests, trying to sound indifferent.

"Why do you say that?"

"Well, you were looking for a bar and you found a bordello. Not exactly the same thing. More interesting in a way, but still…"

I shrug and say nothing, but he does not accept defeat.

"You know, I just want to help you as best I can, and the more I know, the more useful I can be to you."

"I know, Antoine, and I appreciate your help, but I don't even know myself what I'm looking for. Just something important – a serious incident – that happened in the '70s. That could easily be the murder that Tony mentioned."

"We'll know more tomorrow. But you must have an idea of what you're looking for, surely?"

"Not really. It's a subject for a film. We're always on the lookout for stories, you know. Someone gave me a tip-off about this, and I promised I wouldn't reveal anything more about it. Sorry."

"Ah, a film. But if it's got a whorehouse in it, it won't be rated PG, you know!"

"Right, exactly."

Antoine consoles himself by ordering another rosé. In the silence that follows, I attempt to escape my obsessive, circling thoughts. Impossible. I imagine this town half a century earlier. If my parents lived in Issoire, they would have walked across this square.

A brothel! A murder!

At the hotel restaurant, Antoine chooses a table near the window. "Order whatever you like," I tell him. "I'm just going up to my room for five minutes."

The telephone starts ringing as soon as I slide the key into the lock.

"Hello?"

"Why aren't you answering your cell phone?"

"Sorry, Dad. I turned it off on the train and forgot to turn it back on. What can I do for you?"

"Tell me what you're doing in Issoire, for starters."

"But... I already told you about this. I'm scouting locations."

"That's not what they told me at your office. One of the secretaries said you took two days off for personal reasons. She gave me this number."

"Okay. So?"

"So you lied to me."

"*I* lied to *you*! What a joke! And what about you?"

"What about me?"

"Oh, nothing. Forget it. Anyway, what can I do for you?"

"I told you. Explain what you're doing in Issoire."

I am seriously not in the mood for this right now.

"Don't take this the wrong way, Dad, but I think I'm old enough to do what I want without asking for your permission."

"What are you trying to dig up down there?"

"Who mentioned digging anything up? I have business here, that's all."

"In Issoire?"

"Yes, in Issoire. You have a problem with that?"

"What I have a problem with is you telling me lies."

His voice is hoarse and he is carefully enunciating his words. I can easily imagine him right now – eyes blazing, jaw tensed and trembling – and I realize that, even here, protected by the hundreds of kilometers that separate us, I am still afraid of him. It would not take much to make me raise my elbow in front of my face, as I always used to do when he shouted at me.

"You know, Dad," I finally say, "this call is going to cost you a fortune. Let's talk about it when I'm back in Paris."

His aggression has worn itself out. His voice sounds suddenly flat.

"When are you coming back?"

"In two days. Three at the most. I'll call you. I have to go now. Have a good evening…"

I will probably feel guilty about hanging up on him like that, but under the circumstances, I think it is justified.

Thankfully the air-conditioning is on at full blast in the dining room. Antoine has ordered a bottle of Côtes d'Auvergne.

"I took the liberty of ordering a truffade," he says. "It's a local specialty. That way, you won't have come all this way for nothing."

I force a smile.

"What about the town hall, Antoine? Any news?"

"I have the address of the Chat Noir – 15 Rue Desfossés. They went out of business in '74. It's a hairdressing salon now."

"We'll take a look tomorrow."

"And if my friend at *La Montagne* keeps his word, we'll know more about it tomorrow, too. He promised to fax me the information." He gives me an anxious look. "You're not drinking."

"I don't really feel like it. Don't worry about me."

The truth is that I am not sure I would stop at just one glass. And as I want to remain lucid…

Antoine watches me from over his glasses. "You look like there's something on your mind."

I shrug. "Still not feeling all that great. So, you lived in Issoire in the '70s?"

"Yeah, I've never lived anywhere else."

"Did you ever hear about the Bar du Chat Noir?"

"Well, I was a kid back then, but I do think I heard my dad and his friends talking about it. But I don't remember any details. There are always stories about places like that. Do you mind if I ask you something?"

Antoine wants to talk to me about his son. Could I hire him as an assistant on a shoot, at the minimum rate if necessary, just to let him get his foot in the door?

"Tell him to send me his CV. I'll see what I can do."

"Thank you. Commercials are fine, but working on a real movie has always been his dream."

"Do you see him often?"

"We live together."

"Oh, really? How old is he?"

"Almost thirty. We had him late. He'd just found himself an apartment six years ago when his mother – my wife – had an accident. An aneurysm. He decided to stay until she came out of the hospital, but she never did, and he didn't want to leave me on my own."

He nods, eyes closed, as if reliving that painful moment, then he opens them again and smiles.

"And he's still there. He never left. He says that until he meets the perfect woman, he'd rather live with me. What's that smile for? You think it's weird?"

Without thinking, I reach out for the bottle and pour myself a glass of wine. I swallow a mouthful, and then another. Boy, do I envy this man!

"No, not at all," I say finally. "What you went through must have been terrible, but you are lucky, too."

"Yeah, I am."

He takes his cell phone from his pocket, turns it on, and shows me the screen. "Look, he sent me a text earlier to remind me to go see the doctor to check on my high blood pressure. It's like the world turned upside down, isn't it? I'm the one who should be giving him advice."

"You seem to like your upside-down world, though."

"Oh yeah, I'm not going to lie to you. It'll be hard for me when he leaves. We do so much together."

As we eat the truffade – a sort of pancake made with potatoes, lard, cheese, garlic and bacon (Sophie would be horrified) – and Antoine tells me about the renovation of his roof that he and his son have just completed, I find myself drifting into a daydream. I want to ask him simple questions about their everyday life. Do father and son go shopping together? What do they talk about over dinner? Do they ever lose their temper with each other? And, if so, how do they deal with it?

After pushing his plate away and discreetly burping into his napkin, Antoine surprises me by standing up. "Thanks again for Tony," he says. "And for this dinner, too."

"No dessert? A digestif?"

"No, it's very kind of you, but I like to get to bed nice and early. Tony makes fun of me because I fall asleep in front of the TV. He says I've never seen the end of a single movie! So… tomorrow at nine?"

"I'll be there."

Back in my room, I flick through the television channels, searching vainly for something that will distract me from my obsession with the Chat Noir, then give up and call Sophie to wish her a good night. Hearing her voice has often soothed me in the past. The call goes straight to the answering machine, but Lucie picks up as I am leaving a message.

"Hello, Dad!"

"Hi, Lucie. What's going on? Why did nobody answer?"

"I'm talking to a friend on my cell phone. Can I call you back?"

"No, don't bother. Isn't Mom there?"

"She left me a note saying that she was going out to dinner with Claude."

"Claude? The man or the woman?"

'What do you mean?'

"Her bookseller friend or the decorator?"

"No idea. I have to go, Dad. Bye!"

Lying on the bed, hands joined behind my neck, I question my feelings. Would I be jealous if she was eating dinner with a man? The idea is not an unwelcome one.

Chapter Nine

I am finishing my breakfast, seated at the same table as the previous night, when a waiter interrupts my reverie.

"This fax just came for you, sir."

In a few seconds, the emotions blunted by my night of sleep are awakened with a new ferocity. The article, taken from the archives of *La Montagne*, is dated Wednesday November 6, 1974, and is about a police raid. The Chat Noir is described as a brothel, in contravention of the law for the previous twenty-eight years. A fight between two clients was continued outside and a certain Justin Frère, a pharmacist from the nearby village of Orbeil, was stabbed to death with a knife. The culprit was not identified and the Chat Noir was closed for the purposes of the police investigation. The owner and his harem of prostitutes were taken in for questioning.

My chair falls to the floor as I stand up. People at nearby tables stare at me. I know I should pick it up, apologize with a few words or at least a gesture, but all I am able to do is rush out of the room, leaving behind a murmur of disapproval.

In the first-floor toilets, I waver in front of the mirror, wondering if I am about to throw up my porridge, but no, my stomach proves itself sturdier than my heart, and I simply splash some cold water onto my face until I start to feel more human.

Rather than going back to the dining room, I decide to go outside and pace up and down outside the hotel. The temperature is not yet unbearable, the sky is clear, and the flowers and plants in the park offer a serene contrast to the turmoil inside my head.

Finally, Antoine's dusty Golf comes to a halt in front of me and he leans forward to open my door. "Sorry, there was an accident," he explains, before adding that the hairdressing salon on Rue Destossés will probably not open until ten.

In my job, I often have to set up before dawn in order to be ready for the best light, and I long ago learned that the human race is divided into two sorts of people: early birds and those others, like me, who struggle to get going in the morning. The early birds are always full of irritating energy, chattering away uninterruptedly, while we grit our teeth and wish they would just shut up for a minute.

Antoine is clearly an early bird. He talks nonstop about the weather, the traffic, farmers' strikes, a telephone call from Tony, his romantic disappointments with a female neighbor, his dog's arthritis, and various car troubles, all of this without any logical flow to connect it.

"You're not very talkative this morning," he remarks as we park the car.

"I didn't want to interrupt you."

"All the same, you don't look too good."

I hand him the fax from *La Montagne*.

My stomach is so knotted that I wonder if I will ever be

able to untie it. I try desperately to separate this almost half-a-century-old news story from the image of my mother that I carry in my mind. *Mom, Mom, what on earth could you have been doing in a place like that?*

Antoine hands it back to me and asks, "So you still can't tell me what you're looking for?"

"I told you, I don't really know. All I know is that I have to find out more."

He slaps his forehead. "God, I'm such an idiot!"

"What is it?"

Without replying, he grabs his cell phone. I hear only his half of the conversation.

"Laurent, it's me again. Thanks for your fax, but can you do me another favor? I see the article is by Paul Martignac. I never knew him, but the name is familiar. He must be retired by now. Could you check with Personnel to see if they have his address and phone number on file?"

Antoine is silent for several minutes, glancing anxiously at me. "Let's just hope he's not dead," he groans, before suddenly brightening. "Oh, great! Thank you. You've definitely earned that lunch. So, you'll text it to me? All right… bye."

Now we are walking toward Rue Desfossés. It is still early and most of the stores are not yet open. The hairdressing salon at number 15 has a CLOSED sign on its door; in smaller letters below this, the sign promises that Coupe de France will open at 10 a.m. The three-story building – of which the hairdresser occupies the first floor – is unremarkable. It is on the street corner and six windows with black shutters punctuate the dirty beige cement façade on our side. The other façade, on Rue Gustave Jabert, is blank except for two tiny windows with closed shutters. A wrought-iron lantern halfway up the wall is the only decoration.

On the sidewalk opposite, a couple in their fifties are putting out crates of fruit and vegetables. The man is puny and bald, a good head shorter than his big-boned wife. She has an opulent bust and her blue sleeveless blouse reveals a pair of tattooed biceps. Our presence seems to intrigue her for a moment, then she shrugs and goes back inside her store.

"Why don't we go talk to them while we wait for the hairdresser's to open?" Antoine suggests.

We cross the road.

"Do your shopping while we're there," I tell him. "I'll put it on expenses."

I approach the checkout, where the woman is counting change. Behind her, a radio is broadcasting the morning news.

"Hello, Madame. May I ask you a few questions while my friend does his shopping?"

"Depends."

"How long have you been living here?"

"Why do you care?"

"Don't worry, it's not your store I'm interested in, but the bar that used to be across the street. It closed in 1974 and I don't know if it ever reopened."

The woman shrugs her powerful shoulders. "We came here in 2000 and never saw any bar. Before the hair salon, there was a shoemaker there."

"You wouldn't happen to know anyone who has lived here longer, would you?"

Her husband walks over with two shopping bags belonging

to Antoine. "You could ask the old man over there. Come with me."

I follow him onto the sidewalk and discover a strange-looking man half a block away. Dressed in a blue peasant's shirt, he wears slippers on his feet and a soldier's kepi on his head. His long white beard probably makes him look older than he is, but even so, I would guess he is close to eighty. As we talk, he sits down in a folding chair, puts a metal mug next to him on the sidewalk, and rests his hands on the hook of what appears to be a shepherd's staff.

"He's there every day," says the grocer. "Gets here before ten every morning and never leaves until nightfall. Around noon, he comes to ask us if we've got any unsold food, overripe fruit, rancid cheese, that kind of thing. He insists on paying, mind you, even if it's only a few pennies. He always has some change in his pocket."

"What does he do all day?"

"Nothing. Seriously. He watches people, cars. If you ask him a question, he never gives a straight answer. He's not right in the head, if you want my opinion."

"I don't know about that," the man's wife interjects. "Remember the day they announced the death of General Massu on the radio, while he was there? He started ranting about the Algerian War, de Gaulle, and the OAS. He seemed pretty clued in, to me."

"That's true. He did seem to know a lot about it. We couldn't shut him up. But that's the only time."

"Let's pay him a visit," I say. "I'll take two sandwiches – one ham, one tuna – and a basket of cherries. That should loosen his tongue. Oh, and a bottle of beer, too."

"He doesn't drink. He says he can't anymore."

"A Coke?"

"Yeah, he likes that. We give him one for free now and then."

The strange old man sees us come out of the store and he watches as we approach. When we stop in front of him, he leans his head to the side, like a curious bird. His long white hair is greasy, one of the lenses in his glasses is cracked, and there is a smooth triangular-shaped clearing on the left side of his beard.

"Good morning, Monsieur. My friend and I would like to talk with you. Look, we've brought you some food for your lunch."

The old man's hand trembles as he takes the plastic bag and places it on the ground next to the empty mug.

"Do you mind if we ask you a few questions?"

He has still not spoken a word, but his expression is not hostile. He seems content to observe us, the same way he observes passing pedestrians, cyclists, and cars.

"I was wondering how long you've been living here and if you remember the Bar du Chat Noir."

A light glimmers in his gray eyes. I have the feeling that I've piqued his interest.

"Yes, the Chat Noir. Does that ring a bell?"

"A whorehouse," the man says in a voice that seems to come from his chest rather than his throat.

"Exactly," says Antoine. "That's the one. Did you know it?"

The man's silence prompts me to put a five-euro note in his mug before asking again "Did you know it?"

And then, to my surprise, he smiles. He does not have the kind of face that you would imagine capable of smiling.

"Oh yeah," he says. "I used to go there all the time. Even when I only had enough money to buy a drink."

"Did you know a girl named Marina?"

"I don't remember any names. It was a long time ago."

"And the owners? You wouldn't know where they are now?"

"I heard they both died."

"Where did you hear that?"

He shrugs, so I take another five-euro note from my pocket and wrap it around my finger.

"Where did you hear that?"

He sighs, his scruples apparently overcome. "I saw one of the girls recently. She'd become a postwoman. She didn't recognize me, but I never forget a face, even after all those years. I called her over and we talked. After that, she used to stop every day for a chat."

I drop the banknote in the mug and thank him with a nod.

"That postwoman, what was her name? Where could I find her?"

He shakes his head, so I take out my last banknote and carefully smooth it over my palm.

"Nothing bad will happen to her. I just want to talk to her about the Chat Noir."

"Madeleine. She's retired now, but one day she came over to buy all my old books. I used to read a lot, back in the day. I told her about all those books, and she bought them off me for 60 euros."

"Old books? Why?"

"To sell them. She and her husband work the markets."

Several questions, grunts, and shrugs later, it becomes obvious that this is all the information we are going to get.

"Well, we know where to find her, anyway," Antoine says as we walk away. "The market's in Place de la République."

"Is there a market today?"

"Yep. And it's close enough to walk."

The vast open square is occupied this morning by dozens of stands, most of them just trestles supporting a few planks loaded with trinkets, cheap jewelry, wire sculptures, scented oils, old vinyl records (33s, 45s, even some 78s... Dalida, Yvette Horner, Sydney Bechet, Luis Mariano). Many of the stallholders have put up a sort of roof with a tarp to shade them from the sun. An artist wearing a black cape offers to draw my caricature. Tourists mingle with idle locals. Soon, at the end of the first aisle, I spot a white-haired woman and a man in his forties inside a four-sided stand filled with secondhand books.

The woman, whom I hope is Madeleine, is a little overweight. Her face looks drawn. Her hair is knotted in a bun and she wears a long gray smock.

My first question, although rather bland, catches her interest. Yes, she has retired from the post office, but why would I want to know that?

"Actually, Madame, I need your help with something even farther back in time. Could we speak about the Bar du Chat Noir?"

Her face tenses and she shakes her head, but I refuse to give up so easily.

"The subject is important to me for personal reasons, and I am willing to prove my gratitude. How much do you think all these books are worth?"

Madeleine remains unsmiling, but I notice a glint in her gray eyes.

"I don't know… at least eight thousand euros."

I don't believe that for a minute, but what does it matter?

"I will give you a check for that sum and you can keep the books. All you have to do in return is answer a few questions. And, I repeat, I only want to know for personal reasons."

She glances at the man, who is in conversation with a customer. "My son," she whispers. "Not now."

I understand. As Antoine moves away, cell phone pressed to his ear, and as the young man is still busy, I ask her in a low voice "Does the name of Lily mean something to you?"

She raises an eyebrow.

"I'm her son," I add. "I need to know."

She takes her time, staring at me for a long time as if looking for a possible resemblance.

"Ten thousand euros," she says at last.

"Ten thousand," I agree, holding out my hand.

"Come and see me tomorrow morning. My husband and son will be in Saint-Nectaire for the market, so I'll be home alone. Come at nine with the money. In cash."

"I've come from Paris and I don't have that much cash on me. I'll get as much as I can from the ATM and I'll write you a check for the balance. I hope you'll trust me?"

She takes a notebook from her smock, writes a few words on a page, and tears it out.

"Nine tomorrow."

Antoine has finished his conversation and is smiling with satisfaction.

"I have the address and the phone number for Martignac,"

he announces triumphantly. "Shall I arrange a meeting for later today?"

"Sure. I've just had a change of plans."

I call the production company. Yann, one of my partners, answers the phone. "I need an extra day down here," I tell him.

The hint of aggression that I hear in my voice betrays my fear that this is going to end up in an argument, but Yann sounds calm, even a little weary, when he replies "No problem, Philippe. Things are not going well with Charlize anyway."

Paul Martignac lives on the first floor of a two-story house situated at the end of a garden where tomatoes, lettuces, and green beans occupy the space usually reserved for flowerbeds and decorative plants.

The doorbell does not work. We bang on the door several times and finally hear the sound of footsteps followed by a bolt sliding free. The man who answers the door is almost as strange-looking as the one outside the grocery store.

Martignac is a fat old man with rosacea and a rather unpleasant face. He walks slowly with a stick. He is wearing a frayed, plum-colored bathrobe, beige pajama pants, and slippers. The beret on his head is covered in grease stains. The look he gives us from behind his steel-framed glasses is suspicious.

He invites us inside and collapses into the armchair that he had just vacated. He gestures at another, smaller armchair and at a wooden chair heaped with newspapers, magazines, and stacks of paper.

"Sit where you can. Just move that stuff out of the way," he says, pointing at the floor, half-covered with other piles of books and newspapers. A quick glance around the room reveals the most extraordinary collection of heaps of paper I have ever seen. Martignac must read my expression, because he adds "I've had a few girlfriends over the years, but none of them ever stuck around long enough to clean up."

The heat in the room is stifling, and the air is thick with the acidic stench of sweat. I stare longingly at the closed window and our host explains "I can't open it because of the mosquitoes. I don't know what's going on this year."

A cat pushes open a door at the end of the room and I glimpse the corner of a bed. The sheets hang down to the floor. It too is covered with newspapers. The cat jumps onto Martignac's lap and he tells it off "I'm busy, old girl. Why didn't you stay with the others?"

So, there must be a whole family of cats in his bedroom. How can anyone live like this?

"They warned me you'd be coming," says Martignac. "What do you want?"

"I'd like to dig into your memory, if you don't mind. It's about the article you wrote when the Chat Noir was raided by police."

Martignac takes a sheet of paper from his bathrobe pocket and unfolds it. "Yeah, that's what they told me. What are you after?"

"It's really very personal and I find it hard to talk about. I read your article and I could recite every word of it, but what interests me are your memories of that day."

He smooths the page out on his knees, skim-reads it and half-closes his eyes, as if to dive into his memories.

"Write down everything and keep everything – that's the

ABC's of the job," he mutters. He spits on the lenses of his glasses and wipes them with a dirty handkerchief. "Let's see. Yes, that's it. Believe it or not, I can see that whole evening as if it were yesterday. Then again, it was pretty memorable. So… I was in Issoire by chance that evening. I was living in Clermont at the time, but I'd been invited to a friend's birthday dinner. I'd given his phone number to the newspaper, just in case, and that's how I was able to get to the Chat Noir so quickly. Someone had been killed, and my editor wanted my report for the morning edition. The ambulance had just left when I arrived, but the cops were still there."

He pauses and shakes his head. I suppress my urge to pepper him with questions. Better to let him explore the past at his own pace.

"It was my second visit to the Chat Noir. I'd been there four or five years earlier for a bachelor party… for the same friend who I stayed with on the night of the murder, in fact! Anyway, the owner – they called him Popeye because he had an anchor tattooed on one arm – well, Popeye was in perfect health back then, and we chatted, him and me. And this time, I turn up and I see Popeye and his wife Minette answering the cops' questions, except now he was in a wheelchair with a brace around his neck. It was ancient history, one of the girls told me – nothing to do with what had just happened. Anyway, I do my job, I ask questions. The clients all did a runner before the police turned up, but the girls were still there. Well, they had to be – they worked there. Some of them even lived in the bedrooms under the attic. Well, I say bedrooms… they were more like cupboards really! So, they told me about this fight between two drunk clients – they were fighting over a whore, believe it or not! – and then a stabbing at the bottom of the stairs and a second one out on the sidewalk, and the poor bastard, the pharmacist, bleeding out while the other guy ran off. So, I take down the names and I go out to find a phone booth. I call the newspaper with my story and then I go back to the Chat Noir. I was just curious. That thing with Popeye in a wheelchair, with his neck brace, I sensed there was a story there. I wanted to find out more."

Martignac leans forward and picks up a half-empty beer can hidden under his armchair. "Talking is thirsty work," he sighs. "Anyway, so the girls tell me that Popeye was badly beaten a couple of years earlier. His spine was broken. And there was a knife fight, too. One of the girls lets slip that a client was the cause of it all. He got away, but in his haste, he left his bag with all his papers in it. That's how they knew his name. It was a name that a lot of people knew back then. It didn't mean much to her, but I immediately realized I had a scoop on my hands. I went back to the phone booth, all excited, to call my editor with the news, but when I mention the guy's name, I can hear him sort of gasp, and he says that he'll have to talk to the owner about this, and that I shouldn't do anything without his approval."

"So who was this famous man?"

Martignac lifts up his beret and frowns as he scratches his head.

"I'd better not. I still get a small pension from *La Montagne* and I don't want any trouble."

"I see. What happened with your editor?"

"I must have called him back half a dozen times before I finally got an answer: Steer clear!"

"Did he say why?"

"Nope, just not to go near it."

"What about the dead man in your article – the pharmacist?"

"Just a run-of-the-mill local news story. I mean, you read it…"

Sitting in the Golf, I turn to Antoine, who has just started the engine. "I heard you promising a lunch to your friend. How about we invite him to dinner instead, tonight? I have a few questions for him."

"I can call him. What time is your train?"

"Change of plan. I'm staying an extra day."

"But I…"

"I know, you have to fetch Tony. But don't worry, I'll manage. You can take me back to the hotel, and I'll call a cab tomorrow."

"A taxi to Clermont? That'll won't be cheap!"

I pat him on the shoulder. "Don't worry, I'll still have enough to pay you. Give me your invoice whenever you want."

According to Antoine, Chez Juliette is an unpretentious restaurant that serves the best aligot in the region. "Mashed potato with cheese and garlic," he explains. "With a nice piece of meat. Let me know what you think of it."

Yet another recipe that I will not be describing to Sophie.

Antoine's friend, a Breton named Laurent Le Garrec, has already begun the countdown to his retirement. "Three months and seven days to go," he announces happily, pushing toward us the bottle of Saint Pourçain, which is already half-empty. "A few weeks later and you'd have missed me. How can I help?"

"Philippe has some questions," says Antoine.

"Go ahead."

"Martignac told us about a serious incident at the Chat Noir. He said it involved a famous person but he wouldn't give us his name. He said the newspaper's editor had ordered him not to pursue the story. Does any of this ring a bell?"

"It was long before my time. I was still at *Ouest-France* back then, still learning my trade. And then I met my wife, who brought me to Auvergne."

"Are stories often buried like that?"

He drains his glass and asks the waiter for another bottle, then frowns at the ceiling.

"Theoretically, no, of course not. We take our job seriously, but…"

"But?"

"Well, I'd be lying if I said newspaper owners never intervene to rescue the reputation of an influential friend, for instance. It's just human nature."

I am resigned to knowing nothing more about this affair when Le Garrec surprises me.

"All the same, when Antoine mentioned Martignac and the editor's opposition to that story, I did remember an article in some rag that caused a minor sensation a while ago, around the time that I moved here. I don't remember the details, but it was about connections and even collusion between former Resistance fighters. Auvergne had a big part to play in the Resistance, you see. The piece was headlined 'The Law of Silence' and the journalist had made the mistake of using the words 'omerta' and 'mafia' to describe the network of former Resistance fighters. You can imagine the outrage that caused. Insulting heroes, men who'd been imprisoned and often tortured by the Krauts, men who had risked their lives to save France, he was never going to get away with that. I've forgotten what happened to the journalist, and I don't even know why I'm telling you all this, in fact. Although…"

"Although what?"

"It's just come back to me. I remembered that my father had been in the Resistance too, part of a network in Saint Nazaire. Years later, he said that if one of his former comrades asked him to do something, anything at all – I can still hear him saying that very clearly 'an-y-thing-at-all' – he wouldn't hesitate for a second. And he added 'doesn't matter if it's dangerous, illegal, whatever, he could count on me.'"

"I understand. Were there any former Resistance fighters running the newspaper?"

He shrugs. "No idea. But, like I said, Auvergne did its part against the Krauts. There are loads of former Resistance fighters around here. Well, not so many now, I guess, but in the '70s…"

Thankfully, Antoine kept silent during our return journey, giving me time to analyze the day's information.

"Are you sure you can manage without me tomorrow?" he asks as he stops the car in front of the hotel.

"No problem. Send me your invoice and tell Tony to write to me."

"Thanks."

The second half of a soccer game is coming to an end when I look inside the room next to the hotel's dining room. Half a dozen residents are sitting in a semi-circle in front of the television. The tables, though unoccupied now, are still strewn with empty glasses and plates. One wall of the room is filled with bookshelves. Curious, I walk over and start to look through the collection of airport novels and paperbacks left here by tourists. Most of them are what my father would call "bloody romance novels." There is also an old *Who's Who*, a few gardening guides, and a French dictionary covering the letters M to Z.

"I'm looking for something to read too," a woman's voice says. I turn around and see a woman in her thirties dressed in a pale blue Nike sweat suit. She has sandals on her feet. Her blonde hair is tied in a ponytail and she is not wearing make-up. "I can't sleep, and there's nothing on TV, but I remembered that they had some books down here."

I could introduce myself, suggest I help her choose something, even buy her a drink. This encounter could easily be the kind of thing I would later recount to my envious male friends. As it is, I just smile at her. "I can't find anything I want to read," I say, "but it's all a question of taste. Good luck…"

Chapter Ten

After renting a Clio with a GPS, I drive to the address scrawled down by Madeleine, whose surname I still don't know. Located on the outskirts of Issoire, just after a sign for the road to Saint-Yvoine, her house is flanked on one side by a garage and on the other by a sort of single-story warehouse. The house itself is gray, dull, and charmless. The driveway that leads down to the four front steps is lined with crates, trestles, and cardboard boxes protected by tarps. I ring the bell on the gate and Madeleine appears at the top of the steps, beckoning me in. She is wearing a smock like the one she wore the day before, but this time pale blue, and her hair is wrapped in a sort of turban.

I follow her into the kitchen. On the table, covered with a yellow-and-blue check oilcloth, are a pot of coffee, two cups, and a sugar bowl. The décor is simple bordering on spartan, but everything is extremely clean. I begin by thanking Madeleine for welcoming me into her home, but she cuts me off. "Do you have my money?"

I put an envelope containing 450 euros on the table and take out my checkbook.

"There's no problem with the amount – I'm not going back on our agreement – but I need to know your last name so I can write the check."

"Guimard," she says, then spells it out.

There is a long silence after she has poured our coffees. She puts the envelope in her pocket, and I hold the ballpoint pen that I will use to sign the check. We observe each other. She is trying to work out how trustworthy I am, while I try to imagine her face before the years coarsened her features, before her eyes grew gloomy and resigned.

"So, what do you want to know?" she finally asks.

"The Bar du Chat Noir. In the '70s."

"What about it?"

"Did you know someone called Marina?"

She nods.

"I need to see her, to talk to her. Do you know where she lives?"

"No idea. I don't even know if I would recognize her nowadays. We're all a lot older than we used to be."

"I don't even know her last name.'

'We all went by our first names back then, and most of them were false anyway. Me, for example, I was Marilyn."

"And Lily, do you remember her?"

Her eyes light up, and I notice her shoulders stiffen.

"Are you really her son?"

"Yes. I can't say any more than that."

"You have her eyes."

Sensing that our encounter has reached a critical point, I decide to try my luck. After signing the check, I tear it out of the checkbook and push it toward her.

"This is important to me."

She refills our cups—a way of temporizing, I suspect. For my part, I am trying to remain detached. I am here to listen, to note down the facts, whatever they may be. I need to harden my heart, forget for a moment that it is my mother we're talking about. It will perhaps make it easier if we continue to refer to her as Lily rather than Solange.

At last, Madeleine speaks. "Lily was the prettiest of us all. She was sweet and full of life when she arrived. What struck me then was her laughter. She giggled like a little girl and it was contagious. You couldn't help joining."

I don't remember my mother laughing like a little girl. I don't remember her ever laughing very much at all, as a matter of fact.

"She changed over time. I mean she was still sweet, but she sort of retreated into herself after a while. We remained friends, though. I think I was the only one she trusted. She confided once that there was a big difference between what she had done at home and working in a place like the Chat Noir. She hadn't felt dirty before, she said. Now she did. Anyway, what do you want to know?"

"Everything you remember, really. What she told you about her life before the Chat Noir, to start with."

"Before the Chat Noir, you probably know a lot more than I do."

"I don't. Please tell me."

"You know that her mother was single and…"

"Please, pretend that I don't know anything. I really need to hear it from you."

"Okay then. As I said, her mother was single. She went

from one crummy job to the next, until she found an easier way to make a living, entertaining visitors who left money on the bedside table, if you see what I mean."

Now this is my grandmother we're talking about. And she didn't live in a mansion.

"Lily saw her mother with lots of men and she understood what was going on. That's how she grew up, retreating back to her room every time her mother opened the door to men. That may explain how she ended up … I mean we all had different circumstances."

I keep nodding, careful not to interrupt.

"Lily grew to be an attractive young woman. Lots of boy-friends, from what I understood. After her mother passed away, cancer I believe, she met a man, ten years older, I think she said. A travelling Bible salesman. They were planning to get married, at least that's what she thought, but when she became pregnant, the bastard disappeared. Lily could not afford to raise a child. She couldn't even afford an abortion, as a matter of fact. So, naturally, she followed her mother's example, hoping to make enough money before it was too late. Turns out one of her visitors, if you want to call him that, told her about Le Chat Noir. He said that if she joined us, he would talk the owner into lending her the money she needed for the abortion. He would also arrange for a doctor. That's how it happened. I liked her immediately, as I told you, but some of the others called her a goody-two-shoes because there was always some-thing distant about her. Shyness, maybe. It took her a while to pay back the loan, because she didn't work much. Less than the rest of us, anyway. There was this thing about condoms."

"What thing?"

"She couldn't handle the pill. Gave her really bad migraines. That's probably how she got knocked-up by the Bible salesman. When the doctor advised her to stop taking it, she insisted that all her clients had to wear condoms. The boss didn't like it, because the clients would complain, and the other girls, like I said, they thought she was just demanding special treatment. It didn't matter, though, when it happened. Everyone was on her side that day."

"That day? What did happen?"

"Well, there was this one john. Not the usual type – bald, fat, married, you know – no, this guy was young, really well-built, good-looking, and stinking rich into the bargain. He came in from Clermont every month and loved to act the tough guy. One time he pulled out a gun he claimed his father had taken from a Kraut he'd killed. He fired it into a pillow just to show it was loaded. He also liked to show off this knife he carried around on a belt. This guy was a little crazy, we all knew it. Lily must have been with us four or five months when he discovered her. He accused the boss…"

"Popeye?"

"How do you know that?"

I shrug. "Does it matter?"

"I guess not. So, this client – Romeo, as he liked to be called – he made a big scene about it, claiming Popeye had kept his prettiest one a secret from him. Anyway, he paid for her. None of us were keen on going with him even though he was a big tipper. You really had to earn those tips."

"What do you mean?"

"He was a sadist. Sick in the head. He loved to whip us with his belt, but that was nothing compared to the other things he did. He had all these gadgets in his bag that he'd… well, I don't know you well enough to tell you anymore. Popeye would turn a blind eye to all this, not only because of the money, but because this guy's father had connections. It was down to him that the police pretended to believe we were just a bar."

"Okay. So, Lily…?"

"Well, there were a few of us downstairs when she came out of her room in tears, completely hysterical, you know? I can still see her now, crying her eyes out in her pink bathrobe. There was blood pouring down her legs. She was yelling that she was going to call the police. Popeye came out of his office and he grabbed her by the shoulders, trying to calm her down, but she kept shouting that she was going to call the cops. And that's when we saw Romeo coming downstairs, totally calm, with that satisfied smile that we all knew and hated. When he saw what was happening, he took out a wad of cash and threw it on the floor in front of Lily and Popeye. 'Apparently the tip I left on the bed wasn't enough,' he said."

Madeleine turns away from me, to face the window. With her back to me, she says in a muffled voice "It's not easy, reliving moments like that."

Cold sweat trickles down my spine. I grip tight to the edge of the table to stop my hands trembling.

Madeleine stands up and walks over to a cupboard. She takes out a bottle of homemade eau de vie and returns with two glasses.

"I don't know about you, but I need a drink," she says, pouring two glasses.

"Thank you. So… what happened to Lily?"

"She wouldn't let it go. She reached out to the telephone

on the desk and shouted 'Call the cops!' That was when Popeye gave her a couple of slaps and she collapsed onto the couch where we were sitting. As she fell, she banged her head against a wrought-iron coffee table and she started bleeding from a wound in her temple. I had blood all over my bathrobe. We'd never seen anything like this. Popeye grabbed Lily by the shoulders and lifted her to her feet, and he said that if she mentioned the cops one more time, he would knock her out. And he started threatening her with his fist like he was really going to do it, but he didn't have time, because…"

This woman has a gift for suspense. She stops talking for a moment so she can refill our glasses. I shake my head and say "Because what?"

"Because, just then, the kid… well, we used to call him the kid to tease him, but he was the same age as us, in fact, it's just that he looked younger. He was a muscular guy and his job was to guard the door or to persuade any unhappy customers to leave without making a fuss. He was sitting on his stool near the door. None of us could move as this was happening, but when the kid saw Popeye raise his fist, he didn't hesitate. He rushed over and started punching his boss. He only hit him three times before he was on the floor. We had to call an ambulance. We told the police he fell downstairs. He was in a wheelchair for the rest of his life, Popeye, and it was his wife Minette who ran things after that."

"I have a question."

"Hang on, let me finish. If I stop now, I'll lose my thread. So, while Popeye was out for the count and before anyone had had time to call for the ambulance, Romeo gets his knife out. But he doesn't get the better of the kid either. Sure, he cuts his face and there's a lot of blood, but the kid throws a couple of punches and Romeo's on the floor too. He wasn't unconscious, though and he had time to get away before the ambulance arrived. So, yeah, that's how the story ends. And that was the last time I ever saw Lily."

"What do you mean?"

"Well, the kid grabbed her by the hand and they ran off together. I never heard of either of them after that. I can still see them now, through the half-open door, hesitating there on the sidewalk. You know, which way should they go? She was barefoot in her bathrobe. He was holding her with one hand, and with his other he was pressing a handkerchief to his cheek."

"What was the kid's name?"

I know the answer, of course.

"His name? Raoul. Another glass?"

I swallow the clear liquid, which burns like a flamethrower in my throat, then ask her permission to walk around the garden. I need to get some fresh air in my lungs. My body is like a deep-sea diver's, stuck inside a shipwreck, desperate to resurface before his oxygen runs out, but my brain is watching as the final pieces of the puzzle are fitted neatly into place. I am going to need some time to come to terms with the reality, and for now I don't really know what I will do with this information, if I will bury the secret deep within or if... no, I just don't know.

When I come back to the kitchen Madeleine has refilled the glasses.

I sit down heavily in the chair opposite her.

"Thank you for not asking any questions," I say at last.

"You paid me. We're quits."

"What was that bastard's real name? That Romeo guy."

"I knew you'd ask me that. Sablancourt. Jean-Jacques Sablancourt. We weren't supposed to know, but in his rush to escape, he left his bag behind and we hid it to avoid trouble. But we also went through it, of course, and we found all his papers. He called the next day and told us to leave everything at an address he gave us, said he'd send someone to pick it up. We never saw him again either."

"And you never told anyone about all this?"

"We didn't want any trouble."

"I'm the only one who knows?"

"Yeah. Except… hang on, it's coming back to me now. Two years later, there was a fight between two clients over a girl. And one of them ended up dead on the sidewalk."

'The pharmacist?'

"Oh, you know about that? There was an article about the murder in *La Montagne*, and that was the beginning of the end. Minette was starting to get sick of it anyway. Her and Popeye had put enough aside to retire and move south. And that's what they did once the Chat Noir closed. As for us girls, we had to find other jobs. I worked for the post office, and then I met my husband. I was lucky. We make enough to survive. I can't complain. But why am I telling you all this?"

"You were saying that you'd never told anyone about all this, except…"

"Oh, yes! There was an article in the paper. The night of the murder, a journalist asked us lots of questions, including what had happened to Popeye. And that's when one of the girls – I think it was Mitsou, but I couldn't swear to it – anyway, she told him what had happened two years earlier with Lily and the kid…"

"Raoul?"

"Yeah, with Raoul and that Sablancourt guy. And the journalist got all excited when he heard that name. He told us he was going to publish a huge scoop. And that was the last we ever heard of it."

Madeleine sits back in her chair and her shoulders relax. I sense that our interview is over. I am about to thank her and leave, but to my surprise she asks, "If Lily is your mom, does that mean that Raoul is…"

"My father, yes. They got married and they had me."

"And you didn't know about any of this?"

"No, they never breathed a word about it in forty-six years. If my mother hadn't committed suicide…"

"What?" Madeleine exclaims. She drains her glass. "When did that happen?"

"A few months ago. That was why I wanted to find Marina. She found my mother on Facebook and blackmailed her."

"And you want revenge?"

"No, what good would that do? I just want to understand. I didn't know any of this before."

She stares at me, as if trying to come to a decision.

"Could you give me another thousand euros?"

"On top of what I already paid you?"

"For Marina's address."

"But you told me…"

"I changed my mind."

As I sign a check, Madeleine takes a notebook from her smock pocket, tears out a page and scribbles a few words on it. "She's the caretaker of an apartment building. It used to be an old printworks."

Soon after this, I am sitting behind the wheel of the Clio, incapable of thinking rationally or moving a muscle. I am aware that Madeleine is watching me from behind the curtain of her kitchen window. If my parents are not the people I thought they were, who exactly am I?

I stare at the piece of paper that Madeleine gave me. For a moment, out of weariness, or perhaps cowardice, I am tempted just to drive back to Paris and try to forget the whole thing. But in the end, I know that I have no choice.

The light turns green, but a policeman raises his hand and orders me to stay where I am. A funeral procession is passing through. A black cloth hangs from the side of the hearse, embroidered in gold thread with the letter G.

I start to remember – not the procession of cars behind my mother's hearse, but the long walk we took afterward through the central alley of the cemetery in Bagneux. A gentle rain was falling, but neither I nor my father even noticed. Lost in our dark thoughts, we walked side by side behind the coffin, followed by Sophie and Lucie and, behind them, a small group of friends, under umbrellas. Yann, Joe, and Frédéric – my partners and colleagues from Studio Plus – were there, along with Mireille, my assistant. There were a few strangers, too, men and women, whom I imagined must be colleagues of my mother's from the hospital.

I realized later that the smallness of this group was a commentary on my parents' meager social life. While my mother was always open to meeting strangers – "You never know what you might learn," she used to say – my father kept his existence safely locked away. "I've had enough idiots like that in my life," he would grumble. "I don't need any more of them."

I do not remember any dinner parties at our house.

So, there were not many friends at her funeral, but that did not bother me at the time. In truth, I was just trying to get through the day. I did my best to shield myself against my emotions.

A few sideways glances at my father showed him hiding behind a wall of imperturbability. His face was like a balled fist. We walked in silence and I felt simultaneously close to him, sharing the same pain, and incapable of scaling that wall. Finally, the need to show my sympathy won out, and I put my hand on his arm. To my surprise, he put his free hand on mine. That meant a lot to me. I wish I could have opened my heart to him; I wish we could have shared our grief. But soon after that, he took his hand away, and his eyes continued to stare straight ahead.

As we stood next to the grave, as the coffin was lowered into it, as my mother's body disappeared forever, I saw a tear slide slowly down his cheek. I had never seen him cry before. He turned quickly toward me, and his glaring eyes were proof of the anger he felt at being seen in such a moment of weakness. He strode away then, and we didn't see him again that day.

I have no memory of what happened after that. Sophie told me there was a reception at our apartment, but for me a black veil fell over the rest of the day. When my father walked away, I felt as if I truly was an orphan.

The industrial past of this three-story building is easy to discern. In fact, some faded letters on the façade still identify it as the Alphonse & Son Printworks. There is no hint of any physical appeal in its bare concrete or purely functional forms. It is home to a number of apartments now: there are a row of mailboxes in the hallway, and, at its end, a glazed door, the view through the glass blocked by a wrinkled yellow curtain. A plaque on the door reads: Information.

I ring the bell. A hand pushes back the curtain and a woman's face appears briefly behind the window. I get a better look at her when she half-opens the door. Short and thin, she is dressed in a faded pink bathrobe and gray slippers decorated with pink bobbles.

"Yes?"

"Hello, I'm looking for Marina."

"There's no Marina here. What do you want with her?"

"Just to talk, that's all."

She hesitates. I look at her, trying to discern a past dedicated to seduction in that angular face with its pointed nose, tinted glasses, and gray hair. The years have not been kind. Over her shoulder, I see a man sitting on a couch at the back of the room. Wearing a beret, he is leaning forward, wondering who this visitor could be. The right side of his face is frozen into a permanent grimace and one sleeve of his corduroy jacket is rolled up to his elbow.

"Talk about what?" she asks wearily. "I know who you are."

"How?"

"I was told. I saw photographs."

"Who told you?"

"I can't say."

She looks as though she is about to shut the door, so I blurt out "I have not come here to harm you, Madame. I just want to understand. Can we talk for five minutes?"

"What if I don't feel like it?"

"Okay, let's be clear. There is a name for what you did. It's called blackmail. I have enough proof to send you to prison. I researched this, believe me."

She still doesn't move, but I can tell from the tension in her face, the slump in her shoulders, that I have hit the mark.

"If you answer my questions, however, if you help me to understand, I will not take this matter any further. You will never hear from me again. I give you my word."

Slowly she takes a step back, then another, before going over to sit down on the frayed velvet couch next to her husband. She leaves me standing.

"Ask your questions."

"You know my mother committed suicide?"

She does not react.

"You know it was because of you?"

"It was nothing to do with me. It was her decision."

"Why did you blackmail her?"

"You couldn't understand."

"But that's why I'm here."

To prove my determination, I sit on the edge of the table and cross my arms, staring firmly into her eyes. When at last she decides to talk, I have the feeling that what she says is the repetition of a lament heard many times between these walls.

"When the Chat Noir closed, I moved in with my boyfriend. But I wasn't earning anymore, and he changed. He started beating me. One night, he hit me so hard I almost lost an eye, then kicked me out of the apartment. After I came out of hospital, I went to see the cops, but they couldn't care less. As far as they were concerned, I got what I deserved. I had a few jobs, then I bumped into an old client. He'd always been very polite, a real gentleman. He saw my eye and asked me what had happened. Finally, I had some luck. He had an important position at the tax office, and he got me a job. It was during those years that I met Julien."

The man next to her nods.

"He was a foreman in the construction industry. A good job. He earned a decent wage. We got married. And then, unbelievably, in the same month, just two weeks apart, I was forced to retire from my job and Julien fell off some scaffolding and was badly hurt. We were so desperate that it felt like a stroke of luck when we found this shithole. At least I got paid for cleaning work here, and we don't have to pay rent. Anyway, all that to say, life is unfair."

"How did you find my mother?"

"There's a man on the second floor who's always on the road, so I look after his cat for him. He taught me how to use his computer and said I could borrow it whenever I want. And then one day, by chance, I saw a photo of her on Facebook."

"Why did you threaten my mother?"

"Threaten? Well, call it what you want. All I was asking was for her to share what she had. But she didn't want to."

"She didn't have enough money to give you what you were asking for."

"But you do. You're rich."

"That depends what you mean by rich. But anyway, I didn't know. She never told me about your threats. But why didn't you tell her about your troubles? I read your e-mails – you never told her anything."

"I'm not a beggar. I don't want charity. Justice – that's all I want. It's not fair that there are some who have everything and others, like us, who have nothing..."

"One last question," I say, getting to my feet. "If you'd known that my mother was going to kill herself, what would you have done?"

She shrugs. What response was I expecting? There is nothing more for me here.

As I put my hand on the doorknob, her voice immobilizes me.

"You couldn't help us out a little?"

When I would come home from high school, full of rage and obsessed with the idea of revenge, my mother would draw me to her, take me in her arms, and patiently listen to the account of my latest misadventure. I would be mad at a teacher, a monitor, a classmate. I would be set on vengeance over an injustice or an insult. She would let me brood over my plan for a while and then ask me to listen to her. I was the one harmed by such thoughts, she explained. It isn't easy to forgive, she said, but she would like me to do my best.

"Do you promise you will learn to forgive?" she would ask.

"Yes, Mom, I'll try."

The way I stare at Marina before leaving proves that I have failed. I hate that woman.

Chapter Eleven

I am drained as I drive back to Clermont-Ferrand, emotionally exhausted, and all I want to think about is returning to my life, with its solid foundations of Sophie, Lucie, and my job. I daydream about taking Sophie in my arms, about celebrating my birthday and discovering the surprise that Lucie has prepared for me, about working with my crew to set up the first scene of my next shoot.

As I wait at a red light, a doubt suddenly crosses my mind. I pull onto the shoulder and take my wallet from the pocket of my jacket, folded on the backseat. And yes, that mysterious voice in my head was right; I left my credit card at the hotel reception desk after paying my bill. I make a U-turn.

The hotel is deserted, with the single exception of a fat, bald man reading the *Frankfurter Allgemeine* in one of the lobby's chairs. The receptionist smiles broadly when he recognizes me and takes my American Express card from a drawer.

"Could I check the train times? I just missed mine."

"Please use our computer in the television room."

The room is empty, the chairs all tucked under tables, the television off. As I sit in front of the computer, its screen a blur of abstract images, I have an idea, rise and go to the book-shelves, where I pick up the *Who's Who* I saw there yesterday. It is the 2006 edition, but never mind.

I have no difficulty finding the name Sablancourt. There are three, in fact. The first is Sylvain Sablancourt, born November 3, 1920 in Clermont-Ferrand, deceased January 15, 2004. I see that he had two sons, Jean-Jacques and Gérard, the latter the victim of a mountaineering accident in December 1984. A famed Resistance fighter, known as Colonel Jacquain, Sylvain Sablancourt later received various medals for his heroism. After the liberation of Clermont-Ferrand on August 27, 1944, he joined the general staff of the 13th military district. Until his death, he remained actively involved in the regional politics of Puy-de-Dome.

The entry for Jean-Jacques Sablancourt is shorter. Born April 2, 1945, twice divorced, with a son – Gabriel – from his first marriage, his claim to fame was taking over from his father as director of the family plumbing firm, which he sold to the Italian corporation Muscati in 1997. His hobbies are golf and hunting.

His address – in 2006, at least – is Beaumanoir, a village in Saint-Saturnin, Puy-de-Dôme.

As for Gabriel Sablancourt, Jean-Jacques's son, I learn from *Who's Who* that he was born in October, like me, but four years later; that he is married, has a daughter, and lives in Aix-en-Provence.

After making sure that I am still alone, I tear these two pag-es out of the book and stuff them in my pocket. Now sitting in front of the computer, I decide to postpone my research on train times, and instead find Saint-Saturnin on Google Maps.

Fate seems to be smiling on me: this village of 1,200 people is only ten miles south of Clermont-Ferrand. I do not hesitate. I am incapable of resisting. I want to at least see this place with my own eyes.

The name Beaumanoir is emblazoned in gold letters on the two black marble slabs either side of a metal gate. Through its bars, I can see a paved driveway leading to a colonial-style mansion with pillars and terraces. The house is isolated. The closest neighbor – a farm, by the looks of it – is a good thousand feet away, after the sign indicating the entrance to Saint Saturnin.

I press the call button twice, but receive no response. Without any great hope, I push the heavy gate. To my surprise, it opens easily.

The driveway is lined with apple and pear trees. The lawn has been bleached dry by the sun.

Not seeing any sign of life, I hesitate as I place my foot on the first step leading to the terrace. In the end I change my mind and decide to walk around the house before going inside. And that is how I discover the swimming pool – and the man, long white hair covering the back of his neck, sitting in a deckchair. His back is to me, but I can see that he is playing fetch with a white poodle, throwing a tennis ball as far as he can for the dog to chase after and return to his feet.

Next to him on the ground stands an ice bucket filled with bottles of beer. Another beer bottle is in front of him, on a wickerwork table.

To one corner of the swimming pool stands a sort of lamp, with a wire structure on top of it protecting some glowing blue tubes. An electric cable connects it to a socket at the back of the house. There is a constant crackle of incinerating mosquitoes. The ground below is scattered with tiny corpses.

At last I decide to make my presence known.

"Hello!"

The man quickly swivels his chair on one of its legs to face me. The look on his face is hostile.

"Who are you?" he barks. "And how did you get in?"

Despite being over seventy, Jean-Jacques Sablancourt is still a good-looking man. Dressed in garish Bermuda shorts, he is bare-chested and deeply tanned, his body clearly gym-honed. He has regular features and a strong jaw, but his lips are so thin that they are almost invisible. He does not resemble the caricature of cruelty that he had become in my imagination.

"I asked you a question."

"I rang the bell. Nobody answered. And the gate was open, so I…"

"I've told her a thousand times to bolt it when she goes out shopping. She and I need to have words." He sighs and adds "But I still don't know who you are or what you're doing here."

I bow. "My name is Philippe Dubois. I'm writing a novel set in Issoire in the '70s. I want to recreate the past as precisely as possible. Could I ask you a few questions?"

He looks at me curiously, then shrugs.

"All right. It's not like I have anything better to do."

He gestures to a stack of folding chairs, leaning against a wall, and then to the ice bucket. "Pull up a chair and help yourself to a drink."

I sit facing him, but decline his offer of a beer.

"So, go ahead and ask your questions."

"Thank you. My story takes place in a brothel whose name I found in the archives of the local paper. The Bar du Chat Noir."

Sablancourt frowns and his eyes dart to meet mine. His brain has clearly shifted into a higher gear.

"The Bar du Chat Noir?"

"That's right. You know it, don't you?"

"Why would you think that?"

"I happened to meet this woman the other day."

"A retired whore?"

"Sort of, yeah. She gave me your name."

His expression instantly darkens. He tenses like a boxer who has just been hit below the belt. A long moment passes before he composes himself and even manages a faint smile.

"I always thought they'd been through my papers. To be honest, I expected one of them to try blackmailing me. But nothing ever happened. And now, forty or fifty years later…"

"Yeah, it's strange. So, what can you tell me about that place, back in the '70s?"

Relaxed again, he joins his hands behind his head and leans back in his chair, the front feet lifting slightly off the ground.

"Well, I don't want to sound like some old fart reminiscing about the good old days, but… that's what they were. The best days of my life."

"How come?"

He is smiling now, a nostalgic glaze in his eyes, as he revisits a past that, although distant, is still alive inside his mind.

"Everything was simple then. Anything I wanted, any*one* I wanted… I could just help myself. And if they didn't like it…

well, tough shit!' He laughs, his gaze now full of masculine bonhomie. Anyway, with the money I used to leave them, they never complained too much, believe me."

"That's what I heard. Your generosity was legendary, but you really made them earn it, if I've understood correctly. You were rough with the girls, is that right?"

He snorts. "If you want boring sex in the missionary position, you've got your little wifey at home for that. If you want something more special, you've got whores. I'm hardly the only man who likes a bit of rough. Does that shock you?"

"That depends if the special something involves beating women with a belt, or penetrating them with various objects."

He shrugs and raises his voice.

"Don't get all sanctimonious on me! They were whores, like I said. You pay them handsomely, they smile and say thank you. Those were the rules of the game. Or rather, it was a game without any rules. For me, anyway. Yeah, those really were the good old days. If you're looking for stories for your book, you've come to the right man. I know a hundred of them. And they're not fiction, either."

"Does the name Lily mean anything to you?"

As I pronounce that name, I manage to distance myself a little bit, to isolate myself from reality. I have to, if I want to go through with this. Transforming my mother into a fictional character named Lily is like creating a forcefield around me; protecting myself from the raw hurt of the truth.

"Lily! Boy, do I remember her! I guess it was that other whore who mentioned her name?"

"Exactly."

"Lily was a real beauty, but I only had her once. In fact, that was my last ever visit to the Chat Noir. That's the only reason I remember her. I mean, a whore's a whore. Right?"

"So, tell me about her."

"Just a slut like all the rest, except she was younger and prettier. Her thing was playacting."

There is no humor in his laughter. His face becomes a cruel mask as he relives this episode of his past. I have the feeling that he is ignoring me now, talking to himself.

"I did give her a hard time, little Lily. At least my last visit to the Chat Noir was a good one. I had fun with her, to start with. You know what they're like, the snooty ones with innocent faces... butter wouldn't melt in her mouth! But they're all dirty bitches behind the masks they wear. First. I gave her the hiding of her life. Just to warm up, you know. And then I smashed her up inside. Oh God, it was beautiful. If she'd still been a virgin, she'd have bled like a stuck pig, for sure! I bet you anything she still remembers it..."

I do not sense the eruption coming, but it is at this moment that I lose control of my hatred. The forcefield suddenly vanishes. All the methods I have learned to keep my temper in check are helpless in the face of what feels like an explosion.

Sablancourt must see it on my face, because he jumps to his feet as I rise from my chair and stride toward him. But my hands are around his neck before he can defend himself. The man is in excellent physical shape, but I have age and rage – rage especially – on my side. He tries to fight back. He frantically attempts to loosen my grip around his throat, then he starts punching me in the ribs, kicking me in the shins. But I am possessed by a strength that I never even guessed at before. I don't know how long our struggle lasts, but his resistance weakens as his face turns purple, as a hissing sound emanates from his mouth and his eyes bulge from their sockets. Finally, I feel the cartilage snap beneath my thumbs and his body slumps like a sack of bran. I shove his dead weight into the pool and he vanishes under a flutter of bubbles and ripples before rising slowly back to the surface, his white hair like a jellyfish. At the other end of the pool, the poodle – which has, I perceive now, been barking through all of this – lies down and hides its muzzle in its paws, whining feebly.

I stand there panting for several long seconds. The death of this vile man is not enough to calm me down. Gasping for air, I am still trembling with rage. *That's my mother you were talking about, you bastard!* If his body was lying on the ground at my feet and I had a knife on me, I would slash and stab at him until there was nothing left of him but bloody flesh, until I collapsed next to him with exhaustion. I want to spit on his corpse, but it has floated too far from the edge of the pool.

That is when an idea comes to me. I walk over to the mosquito lamp and toss it into the pool. Blue tongues of flame dart over the surface of the water. I have the impression that Sablancourt's body stiffens and shakes a little, but I could be imagining it. I am too full of emotion, too full of fury to trust my own perceptions. Those flames are the equivalent of the knife blade I dreamed of wielding.

A circuit breaker somewhere cuts the current and the pool becomes calm again.

I don't know how much time passes before I begin to recover my composure. If only I could stop my whole body from shaking. I struggle to think clearly. Yes, I know, I have to get out of here without leaving any trace before the help returns.

Acting like a robot, I pick up the chair and the table that were knocked over as we fought. I glance over at the poodle, which has not moved and is still whining, and hurry toward the gate, which I carefully close behind me.

As I drive toward Clermont-Ferrand, I feel as if I am slowly emerging from a dream. I begin to see clearly the reality of what has happened – this murder, which will be part of my life until its very end – but I still feel nothing. It will take time for me to truly understand that I have killed a man. I had vaguely imagined making that bastard confess everything, including his attempt to stab my father. I had wanted to hear him describe the beating he had suffered, but my rage took the words out of his mouth.

One thought alone obsesses me. Going home and being with Sophie and Lucie again. Being part of a family.

Chapter Twelve

"You look pale," Sophie remarks.

As soon as she heard my key turn inside the lock, she came out of our room in her nightshirt, without bothering to put on her bathrobe. I drop my bag on a chair and open my arms wide, but she puts her hands on my shoulders, looking worried, and holds herself at a distance so she can examine me.

"Seriously," she says. "You must have caught something."

"I'm just tired."

She opens a cupboard and pushes me toward the mirror on the inside of the door. "Look at yourself. You're white as a ghost."

"Have you ever seen a ghost?"

"No, you're my first."

She is not wrong. My eyes are sunk inside dark rings and I look gaunt. Haunted. Can a ghost be haunted?

I shrug. "Probably just a cold. You know, going from the heatwave to the air-conditioning in the hotel…"

She stands next to me and I smile at our reflection before taking her in my arms. I kiss the tip of her nose and breathe in her smell. I could never describe it, but I would know it instantly among a thousand other scents.

"Have you eaten dinner?"

"Yes, on the train. I'm not hungry."

She touches my forehead. "You don't have a fever, but you're definitely not well. Let's go to bed."

Later, after we have turned off our bedside lamps, I can feel Sophie – who normally falls asleep easily – tossing and turning beside me. "Did your trip go well?" she asks finally.

"Yeah. Why?"

"I don't know, I just sense something. There's something you're not telling me."

"Well, I met some hot girls and we shared a few nights of ecstasy…"

"I don't think that would leave you pale and shaky."

"Sure it would. That's why I'm so exhausted. Honestly, there's nothing to worry about. Just go to sleep!"

But the peacefulness that I had hoped to find beside Sophie escapes me. Even when I put my hand on her hip – a gesture that has always reassured me, the way my mother's hugs used to when I was a child – I do not calm down.

I think she has finally fallen asleep, until she speaks again.

"I called your assistant to get Marco's number."

"Marco the dresser? Why did you want to speak to him?"

"Not me, my friend Claude. I had dinner with her the other night. She needed advice for some suits in a storefront window."

"Oh, okay."

'So, we chatted for a couple of minutes, Mireille and me. She told me you were in Issoire for personal reasons. And when

I said that I thought you were scouting locations, she started stammering. It was pretty obvious that she thought she'd put her foot in it."

"That's my fault. I forgot to tell you. The scouting was canceled at the last minute, and as I had some business down there anyway…"

"What business?"

"I'm tired, Sophie. You said it yourself. Let's just get some sleep."

But of course, sleep does not come. An eternity later, when Sophie's breathing has at last grown slow and regular, I very carefully lift up the duvet and leave the room. I pad barefoot to the office we share and sit in front of my Mac. The screen's blue glow dimly illuminates the room. I am tempted to google Sablancourt to see if there is any news, but at the last second, I change my mind. I do not want to leave any trace in the cloud.

Three-thirty in the morning is the time for dark thoughts and anguish. I imagine the worst, then try to reassure myself. Could my fingerprints have remained on the shaft of the mosquito lamp after hours in the pool water? But even if they had, how could they identify me? I have never been arrested, after all. Did I leave any other traces of my visit? Could a passer-by have seen my car parked outside the gate? Maybe, but would they really have noted down the license number?

The two pages torn out of *Who's Who* lie on my desk next to my wallet, some cash and my keys. I reread them and my attention is caught by the last of the Sablancourts. Perhaps Gabriel does not know it yet, but he too is an orphan now. Will he grieve like I grieved after my mother's suicide? Will he miss his father as intensely as I miss her.

I am exhausted, but I know I cannot sleep. I open my folder of photographs on the computer screen. There are not many pictures of my parents. Why did it never occur to me that I would need more memories of them? The last photo I have of them is nearly two years old. In that picture, my parents are sitting side by side at the kitchen table. I had been on a scouting trip for a series of TV ads, one Saturday in Place de la Bastille, and I had taken the opportunity to surprise my parents. My father is wearing a brown turtleneck sweater. He was doing a crossword when I arrived, and in the image on my screen he is nibbling the pencil he was using. My mother has not removed the apron she was wearing over a pale blue blouse. She is not wearing make-up. Did I tell her often enough how beautiful I thought she was like that, without any artifice at all? There is a pamphlet open on the table in front of her. A coffee pot and a plate of cookies are in the middle of the table and my half-empty cup is just visible at the bottom of the picture. I didn't even bother to frame the picture properly.

I recognize the brochure that my mother is reading. I had given it to her after two days spent shooting a few scenes for a TV series in a magnificent house not far from Angers. The precision of my memory of this moment takes me aback. I can even reconstruct our dialog that day:

"Take a look at this, Mom. I thought about you while I was there."

"Why?"

"While I was visiting the park, the swimming pool, the tennis courts and the inside of the house, with all that luxury – the tapestries on the wall, the antique furniture – I felt as if I could hear your voice telling me about your childhood."

She smiles, but does not say anything. That photograph was taken a few moments later.

Now my imagination starts playing tricks on me. As I examine those two faces, I find myself in the editing suite, Stefan manipulating the images with the keyboard of his Avid. It always astounds me how profoundly the narrative of a movie can be transformed by cutting a scene at a certain moment or rearranging a sequence of images. Suddenly there is suspense, anxiety turns to hope. For my own part, I know how to transform the nature of a scene by modifying the lighting. My job teaches me constantly to doubt the images I see.

So, I cannot help superimposing on this photograph everything I have learned over the last few days. My father's expression is blank, as usual. Is he paying attention to a fairytale he has heard a thousand times before? Is he happy that I have come to visit? How could I even tell, with him?

And what about my mother? After all these years, has she reached a point where she believes her own fantasies? And, if not, is she ever tempted to reveal the truth to me? Probably not, but it is the beginning of that temptation that I want to read into her shy smile.

When I open my eyes, the digits on my alarm clock spell out 10:21. Groggily, I walk to the bathroom and splash cold water on my face. I am about to brush my teeth when I become aware of the absolute silence around me. There is a note from Sophie on the kitchen table. She has gone out to choose fabrics, and she hopes I'm feeling better. *My man looked like crap when*

he came home last night, she has written, next to a sketch of an exhausted-looking face.

In all honesty, I am relieved to be alone. It is so much easier not to have to sidestep her questions.

I did not eat dinner on the train last night and I am starving. In the refrigerator, I find a box of eggs, some grated cheese, and two slices of ham. There is a half-baguette in the breadbox.

I had been vaguely intending to go to the production office, but when I come out of the shower I realize I have more important things to do.

I put on a pair of jeans, a tee-shirt, and a leather jacket and leave a note to let Sophie know that I'm feeling much better, then I go out to find my motorcycle, which is parked outside a building at the end of the street. I pull out into traffic. The wind in my face makes the heat bearable.

Outside the cemetery in Bagneux, people are selling flowers and wreaths. I choose a bouquet of white roses, my mother's favorites. I have kept a note of her grave's location on my phone, and I find the Avenue des Érables Planes on the map near the caretaker's cottage.

This is the first time I have visited my mother's grave since the funeral. I never felt the need before. Visits to cemeteries have always struck me as an exercise in futility; what is the point? Today, however, there is nowhere else in the world I would rather be.

Her gravestone is a plain gray marble rectangle, no more or less remarkable than the hundreds of others in this aisle. I lean down and caress the name of Solange Lamont, engraved in gilt lettering, then place the roses on the ground below.

There are not many visitors here, and the few I can see are

quite distant. I am glad; I want to spend a moment in peace with my mom, and I don't have to worry about drawing curious looks when I sit down on the gravestone.

But the moment I touch the marble, it is as if my brain freezes: no thoughts come, and I am trapped inside a dark bubble where all sensations, reflections, and perceptions are foreign and excluded.

After a while and without warning, I am shaken by a terrible vibration that rises through my chest, expands to my shoulders and makes my jaw tremble as tears stream down my face. I am filled with pain, but also relieved to have come back to life. Thankfully, there is no one around to witness my display, and I am free to sob my heart out unselfconsciously. God, how it hurts! God, how I miss my mother!

Slowly, effortlessly, I calm down. I feel drained but lucid. Words escape my mouth in a whisper, although I am barely even aware that I am speaking *Mom, why didn't you tell me anything? Why? Why? I wish I could have loved the real you, not a character from a novel. Why wouldn't you let me know you the way you truly were? Did you think I would be less proud of you, that I would have loved you less? But Mom, you know I adored you! You have no idea how much I miss you. I feel terrible admitting this, but I am mad at you too. It's true: I can't accept that you chose to leave me.*

I stand up and take a few steps, breathing deeply, relaxing my tensed muscles, before sitting down again. I have never believed in an afterlife, but I feel the need to cheat for an instant and to convince myself that my mother can hear me. I have to let these words out or they will damage me inside.

It hurt me so much when I said goodbye to you here, but not until today have I been able to cry. I built a wall around my heart to keep the pain away, but that wall collapsed when I killed the man who abused you, and who insulted you all those years later. I am not proud of what I did, but I feel no remorse – none at all, you hear me? – and I am going to live with it. All the same, it was only when I killed that man that I was able to release all this pain.

A family walks past, an elderly couple dressed in gray and a little girl walking sulkily behind. She glances at me curiously for a second then turns away as I wave at her.

You know, it occurred to me on the train that I no longer have any right to condemn Dad for his violent nature, because it was that violence within him that saved you back then. And it is that nature – which I inherited from him – that finished the bastard off, forty years later. The same man, punished by your husband and your son.

I kiss my fingertips and stroke the letters that spell out my mother's name.

Okay, I'm going now. I'll come back soon to talk with you again. Goodbye. I love you, Mom.

Lucie was in her bedroom with a friend when I got home. It was late in the afternoon. I had driven around the beltline several times, trying to escape my thoughts. Now the four of us sit together in the kitchen for dinner: a leek and mushroom quiche from the vegetarian deli. The two girls monopolize the conversation, which is fine by me. Sophie is more involved than I am, but I can read her anxiety in the frequent glances she shoots at me. I do my best to reassure her with a smile, a wink.

"Dad! Jennifer asked you a question!"

"Oh, I'm sorry, Jennifer, I was thinking about work. What did you say?"

"I was just asking what Auvergne is like. Is it worth visiting? Issoire is in Auvergne, right?"

Later, as I am waiting for her in our bed, Sophie comes out of the bathroom in an alluringly short nightshirt that I have never seen her wear before. I know every inch of Sophie's body, but seeing her like that awakens my desire. I lift up the sheets for her and ask "Are you trying to seduce me, Mrs. Robinson?"

"Why not?"

She quickly nestles in my arms.

"It feels good to be with you again," I say, running my hand from her shoulder down to her hip.

She responds with a sigh that soon turns to a sort of purr as my hand moves between her thighs. But when Sophie caresses my stomach, I pull away.

"Just a second."

She tenses and moves back, staring at me intensely. "What?"

"I want you – I want to make love to you – but I have to tell you something first."

I talk quickly, desperate to remove the cloud of anxiety that is darkening her eyes.

"The reason I went to Issoire is that I was trying to understand what could have led my mother to... well, you know."

"What are you...?"

"Hang on. I recently discovered that it was in Issoire that my parents first met. They never told me about that period in their lives and I wanted to find out more. I can't tell you more than that now. One day, perhaps, but not yet. Please don't blame me; this is a very painful subject for me. I am telling you this now because I don't want to have to keep lying to you. I swear on my life that none of this has anything to do with you or with us. Do you understand?"

"I'm trying."

"All of this is about my parents, about me and the past. I have to reconstruct myself. I need time."

"I can keep a secret, you know."

"I know. It's just that I'm not yet ready to put words to what I've learned. I have to speak to my father about this. All I'm asking is that you trust me. I love you. I hope you don't doubt that."

Sophie presses her lips against mine, then teases me with her tongue. Soon she has stripped off her nightshirt and is opening her arms to me.

"Take me."

I move inside her.

Later, Sophie is lying on top of me, her head on my chest. She lifts her chin and asks, "What's so funny?"

"I didn't laugh."

"I felt you smile. I have a sixth sense, remember."

"I was just thinking about something this guy said to me recently, that having sex with his wife was boring. I've just realized that there is nothing better. When I'm inside you, I feel like I'm home."

She smiles. "I wouldn't want to meet your friend."

"He's not my friend."

I might have added that she is unlikely ever to meet him.

Chapter Thirteen

We fell asleep peacefully, hand in hand, but I awoke soon afterward and spent the rest of the night haunted by the prospect of going to see my father. Unable to calm my fears, I invented various scenarios for what I imagine will be a confrontation. Who will open fire first? Will he demand an explanation for my presence in Issoire, or will we play a sort of poker game, with him trying to force me into revealing my hand? Will I ever be able to free myself from my father's shadow?

At quarter to six, I give up trying to sleep. Without waking Sophie – whose alarm will ring in an hour anyway – I get up and take a shower. The daylight soothes the anxiety that has tormented me all night, but I still don't have a clear vision of what to expect. We'll see, I suppose.

As I ride through congested traffic on the beltline, I think back to the first time I took this road with my father. Back then, my most pressing desire was to rediscover my childhood, my adolescence, to rekindle a connection that the years had worn away, to clear up the misunderstandings between us. And, of course, to understand what had pushed my mother to end her life.

When I arrive at the Résidence Bellevue, I hesitate. I don't like the idea of announcing my presence at the reception desk. I am not a visitor, I am here to see my father. It's a question of principle. So, I take the elevator to the sixth floor and follow the worn-looking beige carpet along the corridor.

A surprise awaits me outside my father's apartment door. The breakfast tray on the floor contains two empty cups, two glasses of orange juice, two plates, and two rolled-up napkins, plus a basket filled with triangles of toast. It takes a moment for me to translate into thoughts what my eyes are seeing. I raise my hand toward the doorbell, then let it fall without ringing. *Think, Philippe! Just take a moment to let this sink in. Better to go back downstairs for a while…*

The elevator arrives and a man in his thirties comes out. I don't really look at his face, but in the corner of my eye I see him dialing a number on his cell phone. As I wait for the doors to close – they are programmed to be slow, for the sake of the aged residents – I hear this stranger call out "Helloooo!" in a high-pitched voice. My heart leaps. I have heard that voice before. It takes me a moment to locate the memory, but instinctively, without thinking about it, I get out of the elevator and follow the man from a distance as he walks through the corridor and stops outside my father's room. By now I know – yes, I'm certain – that that voice is the one I heard on the telephone the first day I was here, when I said I was Raoul Lamont's son and he hung up.

The stranger continues his conversation. He has not seen me. I press myself against a door marked STAFF ONLY. He is speaking to a woman he keeps calling "my lovely," and it sounds as if he is trying calm her down. Several times he repeats that he "will explain everything." I see him from behind and occasionally in three-quarter profile as he hops from foot to foot. He is not particularly tall and has narrow shoulders, and he is dressed in a black short-sleeved shirt and a pair of pale canvas pants. He wears a black kippah.

At last he hangs up and curses softly before ringing the doorbell. A few moments later, the door opens. I cannot see who it is that welcomes this visitor, but I hear him say "Hello Mom," and then he disappears.

What happens next is not the result of a decision on my part. Something inside me urges me to rush across the few yards that separate me from my father's room and block the door with my foot before it bangs shut.

I push it open and now I am in the presence of a woman with gray, shoulder-length hair, dressed in a pale blue flannelette bathrobe and a pair of matching slippers. Behind her I see my father in his pajamas, sitting in his favorite armchair, which he insisted on bringing from the old apartment. He is wearing the same thick-striped pajamas he has always worn.

He is about to get to his feet when he sees me and falls back into his seat, staring at me with stupefaction.

I realize that it is a cliché to compare the moments that follow this with one of those slow-motion scenes in a movie, many of which I have helped produce over the years, and yet that is exactly how it feels as my gaze moves around the room and its occupants and their eyes meet mine.

One thing is clear, the woman who turned to my father as if to await his instructions has no doubt about my identity. As soon as she saw me, she knew who I was.

The visitor who came in before me, however, looks lost, completely baffled, as his mother raises a hand forbidding him to react physically to my intrusion. The way his mouth opens and then closes without making any sound puts me in mind of those fish that stare out from behind glass in aquariums.

The bedroom door is ajar and I can see the edge of the unmade bed.

My father looks as stunned as most of his opponents probably looked in the boxing ring when he was young. Slumped in the armchair, he stares disconcertedly at me. I don't remember ever seeing him at such a loss before.

My father's girlfriend must once have been pretty – she has beautiful dark eyes and a finely shaped mouth – but age (she must be at least sixty) has thickened her features; her hair is a mess and her face looks drawn. Given that she has just got out of bed, I suppose this is understandable.

I also make a physical inventory of the room and spot the ball of brown wool, the knitting needles on the table, next to a cookery book, its page marked by a paper knife, and a black leather handbag with a glasses case poking out of it. There is a stack of newspapers at the foot of my father's chair.

It is the stranger's voice that brings the movie of my life back to normal speed.

"This is nothing to do with me," he says in his falsetto voice. "I didn't even know he was behind me."

As the woman shrugs, apparently resigned, he changes his tone and remarks "You're not even ready, Mom. We're going to be late."

She nods and announces that she is going to get ready now, that she will be back in five minutes. But as she picks up her handbag, I call out, "Aren't you going to introduce us, Dad?"

He really is out for the count. His voice sounds weirdly weak as he says, without even bothering to get out of his chair "Janine, Daniel, this is my son Philippe."

Janine holds out her hand, which I shake, and the two of us nod at each other. As for Daniel, he seems more interested in his shoes, which could do with a shine.

"All right, well, I'm going to get ready," Janine repeats, beckoning her son to follow her.

Alone now in the living room, my father and I tacitly decide to wait in silence until Janine and Daniel have left the apartment. I stand in front of the bay window and stare at the rusty, graffiti-strewn train carriages below. Behind me, I hear my father's wheezy breathing. I hadn't noticed it until this silence. He is obviously keeping up his bad habits.

My cell phone purrs inside my pocket. Sophie is wondering where I am. I respond and end my message with a smiley-face emoji. She can interpret that as she wishes.

I hear footsteps on the floor and turn around. Janine is now dressed in a pale green pantsuit and looks more presentable. Daniel's expression is still hostile.

"See you later," says Janine to my father, then adds: "I'll call you."

Turning to me, she smiles warmly and says: "It was nice to meet you." Daniel is already on his way out of the door.

At last we are alone. "Give me a moment," my father says. "I'm going to get dressed." I know him well: in his pajamas, he feels at a disadvantage.

As he walks away in a pair of Persian slippers that I have never seen him wear before, I notice that my father is dragging his feet. His back is bent, too. Is this just an impression, or has he aged in the few weeks since moving here?

When I look around, I feel that I am standing in an unfamiliar world. Of course, we are no longer in Rue de la Roquette, but there is more to it than that. I am a stranger in a foreign land. My father has always been an extremely orderly man – a mania I have inherited from him. So many times, I have seen him adjusting the silverware at the family dinner table. I will never forget his anger when I would go to bed after leaving a book open on the table or a sandal under the couch. And now... look at this place: the knitting, the cookery book, the half-empty glass of orangeade on the table, the newspapers on the floor, a scarf draped over a half-open cupboard door. And inside that cupboard, a chaos of shoes and umbrellas that, in my youth, would have drawn forth a shower of insults, sometimes even blows. I will never feel at home here.

My father is back, and he is ready for battle now. I can tell this from the tone of his voice, the way he holds his shoulders and his chin, the blaze in his eyes. He grabs a chair and turns it around so can sit facing me, with his arms crossed on the seatback.

"So?" he says.

"What do you mean, 'So?'?"

"What do you want to know?"

"I don't really know where to start."

"I'll start, then. What the hell were you doing in Issoire?"

I hesitate for a moment, like a soldier with a grenade in his hand. Am I going to take out the pin? Well, what choice do I have?

"I went to find out about the Chat Noir."

He must have been expecting something like this, yet he looks utterly dumbstruck.

"What? What were you…"

"Please don't interrupt. You asked me a question, I'm answering it. I received an anonymous e-mail advising me to investigate the Bar du Chat Noir and the way my parents met each other."

"There's no such thing as an anonymous e-mail."

"Of course there is! It was a fake account, just a jumble of numbers and letters. I replied several times, but without response. So, I wanted to be sure. I took the train down there."

"Without telling me. Without even speaking to me."

"First, I wanted to find out if it was serious. Why bother you, if not?"

"All right, I'll let that go. So?"

"I went to the town hall and found the address of the Chat Noir, which has not existed for a long time. I learned that it was not really a bar – I don't need to explain anymore, do I? I spoke to some of the neighbors, and finally I got lucky; I was put in touch with one of the women who used to work there, and she told me everything."

"What was her name?'

'She made me promise not to tell anyone. But she remembered the pretty Lily and the man they all called the kid, and the night the two of you ran away together."

My father puts his hand to his chest, and I take a step toward him. He pushes me away. "I'll be fine," he says brusquely.

In the tiny refrigerator, I find a bottle of mineral water and pour it into a glass.

"Here, Dad. Have a drink."

I give him time to get over his shock.

"Are you feeling better?"

He nods, inviting me to continue.

"That woman told me about the night when you defended Mom before running away with her. She remembered it all like it happened yesterday. Although I guess it is the kind of thing that nobody is likely to forget. I was proud of you when I found out how you wiped the floor with your boss and that piece of shit Sablancourt."

"How do you know his name?"

"That woman remembered it."

"All right. So… what's your problem?"

"It bothers me that you lied to me all those years."

"Lie! Did I really lie? It's a bit more complicated than that. And anyway, it was your mom who wanted it that way. She preferred the past that she invented herself. And I didn't see a problem with that. In fact, I thought she was right. And I still do. What harm did that 'lie,' as you call it, actually do?"

"It prevented me from really knowing you. Especially Mom, when I imagine the pain she went through. I just wish I could have…"

"Could have what?"

"Helped her, if possible. Told her I was proud to be her son. Maybe then she wouldn't have… well, you know."

My father shrugs and mutters a few words that I do not grasp. Although I have the vague impression that one of them is "nonsense."

"So, can I ask a few questions now?"

He shrugs again.

"Why don't you start by telling me about Janine, Dad?"

"I don't have to answer to you. But what do you want to know?"

"How long have you known her?"

"Six years."

I whistle between my teeth. "Six years! Jesus.... Did Mom know?"

He shakes his head vigorously.

"You didn't love Mom anymore?"

"Of course I did. And I would have done anything to stop her swallowing those pills if I'd have guessed what she had in mind. But it's true that our marriage was past its best. Time can do that to anyone, apparently, and there's nothing you can do about it."

"But you loved her so intensely, didn't you? You were crazily jealous, I remember that."

He nods, frowning, and during the long silence that follows, I have the impression that he is looking deep within himself. He takes a breath, balls his fists, hunches his shoulders, and leans forward, eyes lowered. All of these are signs that I have learned to read as presages that he is about to make a difficult decision. As he once told me, he is, above all, a "physical man."

"All right," he says finally in a blank voice. "As you want to know..."

He takes his time, and looks up at me as if inviting a response. But I know that the slightest wrong word or gesture at this stage could ruin everything, so I stay silent. He nods.

"This is not my kind of thing, but... well, here goes. I've thought about this a lot since she left us. It's strange, the way we live these damn lives of ours. I remember that I never judged her back then, when she used to take clients up to the second floor. I was already in love with her, secretly, but – and if you don't believe me, that's your problem – I wasn't jealous. It hurt me, but I understood that we had both been fighting to survive. I'd been involved in a few robberies, here and there, but…"

"What? Robberies! But you've never told me that before…"

"I was hardly going to brag about it. Anyway, better to let bygones be bygones."

"Fair enough. So, you robbed banks?"

He snorts. "Not banks, no – you've been watching too many movies. There was a gas station, a grocery store, a hardware store… just small stuff. Me and a friend. I was a young idiot, just struggling to prove to myself that I really existed, that I wasn't just a nobody…"

"Was that why you boxed, too?"

"Yeah, boxing gave me an ambition, taught me discipline, and it led to me getting that job at the Chat Noir. Plus, as soon as I started boxing, I gave up being a criminal. But anyway, I didn't like what your mother did, but I understood it. She had to survive, just like me. She didn't really have much choice. But why am I telling you all this?"

"You were talking about jealousy."

"Oh yeah. I don't know why I was like this, but while her work at the Chat Noir didn't really bother me – the past was the past, and I could draw a line under it – from the moment we started living together, from the moment we got married and had a normal life, I became sick with jealousy. She'd smile at some guy in a bistro and I'd go into a rage. She'd answer the phone at home and I'd run to pick up the extension. I even steamed open her letters, if you can believe it!"

I certainly can believe it. I refrain from mentioning the incident that kept us apart for almost two years.

"The idea that she was cheating on me made me want to murder someone," he sighs.

"Double standards," I murmur.

"What? What did you say?"

"Nothing. Forget it."

"If you're talking about Janine, it's not the same thing. You weren't living with us anymore and we didn't tell you everything, but your mother's depressions were hard on me. I felt like I was suffocating. So when, by chance, I met a woman who made me laugh, who looked on the bright side of life, I was easily tempted."

But it wasn't Janine I had been thinking about; it was the red-headed cashier I had once seen him kiss.

"She's a good woman, Janine," he remarks, before exploding "What now? What's so funny?"

"I was thinking about her son. Bit of a giveaway, that skullcap. So, she's Jewish?"

"Yeah. So?"

"Oh, nothing. I was just remembering some of your diatribes. The queers, the towelheads, the kikes…"

"Yeah, well… That just proves that I can make an exception."

"Ha, you're not kidding! Where did you meet her?"

"At the supermarket. Your mom was in hospital and I was grocery shopping. I was reading the description on a frozen microwave meal – something Greek with eggplant – when I heard a woman's voice saying, 'That's a really delicious recipe, but it's a shame to eat it out of a packet. Homemade is so much better.' I replied that my culinary talents were limited to hard-boiled eggs and warming up cans of soup. That's how it started. She's a fantastic cook, Janine. She invited me to eat dinner at her house with her husband, who was very ill – he had cancer. We became friends, she taught me some simple recipes and, you know, little by little..."

"I see. And the husband?"

"He really wasn't well. That's why they bought an apartment here, on the floor above, so he could have permanent medical assistance. But very soon after they moved in, his condition worsened. He died in hospital six months later."

"And Mom never suspected anything?"

"I was careful. I wanted to live a little, but I didn't want to hurt her."

"Okay."

"I was listening to the radio the other day and I heard something that really struck me as true. This guy, about my age, said that as he entered the winter of his life, he'd really hated the weather. So, when a ray of sunlight appeared, he decided to make the most of it. That's what I did."

A voice inside me advises me to wait a few years before I judge him.

Shaking his head as if he's just come out of a pool, my father decides to change the subject. His smile is a marked contrast to the pensive look he's worn for most of this conversation.

"Daniel is an arrogant asshole, if you want my opinion, but Janine is really a remarkable woman. I'd like it if you could make an effort with her. You think you could?"

"I'll think about it, Dad. You have to understand—this is quite a lot to take in. I'll need a little time."

"I see."

"I'll come back to see you – and I'll let you know in advance next time – but first I need to take a step back, get used to…"

"I understand. Take your time."

I lean forward and kiss him on both cheeks. I do not want to forget that he is my father.

I have left the building and am walking quickly toward the parking lot when a thought stops me in my tracks. Its power is such that I am frozen in mid-stride. I turn around and instinctively look up to my father's window. I realize that he must possess the answer to a question that I cannot ignore. I have to know. How else can I go on living?

Back in the lobby, I sit on one of the fake leather benches. I need to find an oasis of calm inside my head. Organize my thoughts, try not to dramatize this before I have found out the truth.

I don't know how much time passes like that, my mind prey to a whirlwind of thoughts, but when I finally get hold of myself, I know that I have no choice. I must confront my father once more.

"What now?" he asks exasperatedly when he answers the door, but I refuse to back down.

"Sorry, Dad, but I have an important question."

"Go ahead."

"Can I come in?"

We are sitting face to face now and the tension between us is palpable, as if my father has already guessed that we are about to cross a minefield.

"I imagine you remember the date that you fled the Chat Noir."

He raises his eyes to the ceiling. "Some things you never forget. February 17, 1972."

"Okay, second question. I hate saying this, but I need to know. Mom didn't use the pill, right?"

"How do you know that?"

"That woman told me everything,"

"The pill gave her migraines."

"I know. She made her clients wear a condom."

"Yeah. So?"

"That guy, Sablancourt… you think he used one?"

My father laughs coldly.

"That bastard? I'm certain he didn't. It was almost a question of principle for him. You should have seen how he treated them all. He said he paid them well enough to put up with anything."

"Hang on. Before that day, had you and Mom ever been together? I mean, had you ever… don't make me say it."

"No. I was kind of in love with her. Well, okay, I was completely in love with her. But no, I just admired her from a distance."

"And after you ran away, when did you start… making love?"

"For God's sake, why the hell would you want to know that?"

"I'm serious, Dad. Please just trust me and answer the question."

"All right. We waited a few days, because that son of a bitch had really hurt her."

"A few days?"

"I don't remember exactly. Maybe a week. Are you going to tell me where you're going with all this?"

"It's simple, Dad. Well, I guess it's not simple at all, but anyway… I was born eight and a half months after you left Issoire. Are you certain that you're my father?"

He nods for a long time, then points toward the kitchen. "I know it's early for a whisky, but I think I need one right now. There's a bottle in the cupboard. Would you pour me a small one, with lots of ice? That would help. Have one yourself too, if you like."

I return with one glass, which my father sniffs before swallowing a mouthful.

"We talked about this a lot back then," he says finally, "your mom and me. If she'd wanted to get an abortion, it wouldn't have been easy but she could have done it. I was in favor of the idea, but she refused to even think about it. She was certain that her baby was mine. Women know these things, she kept saying. What could I say? It was her decision, right? So, in the end we agreed that we would never know for sure and that it didn't matter. The baby inside her would be our child. We never talked about it again after you were born. I can't speak for her, but I know that I never even thought about it after that, not even when I was half-crazed with jealousy, not even when you were giving us a hard time."

He swirls the ice cubes around his glass and swallows another mouthful.

"Anyway, DNA tests didn't exist back then."

"They exist now."

"Don't tell me you want to know."

This is precisely what was occupying my mind a moment before.

"No, Dad. I don't want to know."

Being a murderer is a burden of which I will never be free. I do not feel strong enough to carry an even heavier one.

I'm putting on my motorbike helmet when I feel my phone vibrate in my pocket. Sophie.

"Hi honey, what's up?"

"It's Lucie," she says. "She's been dumped by François and she's inconsolable. She's gone off to her room, I can hear her sobbing away, but she won't let me in. To make things worse, she has to prepare for that math exam tomorrow and well, me and the math you know ..."

"I'm on my way."

CPSIA information can be obtained
at www.ICGtesting.com
Printed in the USA
BVHW072342020321
601492BV00005B/426

9 781977 234643